The Crystal:

The Legend of
Hunter Hogan

Published by
Books for the Nations Publishing
ISBN 979-8-9919089-2-4

Part 1: Light
"The dawn of a Legend"

Chapter 1

Hunter squinted his eyes as the sun peeked out from behind a cloud and refracted through the windshield. He pulled his sunglasses down from on top of his head, bringing the mountainous landscape and windy road back into view.

He and his family were on one of their favorite types of outings; they were going camping in the rockies. It was the third week of August, and they planned to spend the entire week there before the school year started back the next week.

Hunter was riding in the family's Jeep, bouncing down the bumpy back roads to the campsite. In the driver seat was his older, 16 year old brother, Trent.

Trent didn't really follow the rest of the family in their need for adventure. He often preferred less physical, and in his opinion, less dangerous forms of entertainment.

In the back seat, were Hunter's best friends: Brady Skott and Austin Martin. They were both on the baseball team with Hunter.

Brady was a bit more reserved. Often the voice of reason among the friends. Austin and Hunter were, at times, a bit too adventurous for their own good. Brady on the other hand, was a more cautious person, often keeping the other two out of trouble.

Hunter had brought them along in hopes that they would get to go "off trail" hiking for a few days during the trip. Trent and Hunter's mom, Grace, hated going off trail. His dad, Jack, didn't really mind, but Hunter always got outvoted when it was just them. He hoped, with his friends along, they would at least get to break off from the others for a few days.

Staying on the trail was just so basic for a 13 year old boy approaching his Freshman year. It wasn't "cool" enough.

Hunter looked in the side mirror at his mom's SUV trailing behind him. He could see his dad driving and his mom in the passenger seat. She was squished against the dash from all the luggage crammed behind her.

They had been driving from Boulder Colorado to the Rocky Mountain National park for about an hour and a half. Now, they were finally nearing their destination.

They were on the final stretch of road to their camp site. The views had been stunning on the way in. The mountains peaked on both sides of the road, creating steep ridge lines and deep valleys. Natural lakes dotted the area. Each one they passed had wisps of steam rising from it as the warmer water met the cool morning air. Pine trees filled the landscape, casting long shadows in the morning sun.

After about an hour's worth of driving, they arrived at the Glacier Basin campground. The boys, except for Trent, squirmed impatiently in their seats, as the car drove through the various campsites. Hunter eyed the landscape anxiously from his seat, looking for their pad, #28.

The entire campground was seated in a valley and surrounded by mountains on every side. Though there were cars and tents and RVs, the landscape made him feel as though he really was cut off from civilization. Trent felt that way for another reason.

"Ugh," he tossed his phone aside, "Why don't they put a cell tower out here?"

"Because that would defeat the purpose of camping," Austin informed him from the back seat.

"Well, I can't find the campsite without the GPS," he complained.

"28," Brady called, leaning up between the front seats and pointing, "I see it right over there."

"Who needs a GPS?" Hunter remarked.

Trent grumbled as he pulled into one of the parking spaces by the wooden post marked "#28". In front of them were two pads for setting up tents, a charcoal grill, a firepit, and a long picnic table.

Hunter's parents backed into the parking lot beside them. "Alright Trent, go entertain yourself with a stick or something," Hunter mockingly suggested as he opened his door.

Everyone else followed suit, only Trent did so with a bit more attitude than the rest.

"How was the drive?" asked Hunter's mom as she squeezed out of her seat.

"Same as always," Hunter replied, shrugging his shoulders.

"Amazing," Brady added, giving a bit of a warmer answer.

Trent and Austin walked around from the other side of the Jeep. "Boy's, come help me unload all this!" Hunter's dad called.

They all walked to the trunk of the SUV. Trent, not thinking, walked around and immediately flung open the trunk. As his hand touched the handle, his dad called out, but it was too late.

The trunk opened and the contents spilled out onto the ground. "Trent!" the group said in only lighthearted annoyance.

"Sorry," he said, drawing out the word and throwing up his arms, "I didn't pack it!"

Everyone smiled and began to load up their arms and carry the supplies to the campsite. There was way too much according to Hunter's standards. He would rather just rough it with little to nothing, but that's not how his mom saw it.

She prepared for warm, cold, rain, and shine. There was nothing nature could throw at her that she hadn't already prepared for.

They had also packed two tents: one for the kids and one for the couple. Hunter had brought along some hammocks and his survival backpack, which consisted of a few hunting knives, lours and fishing line, bear spray, firestarters, and first aid.

Despite the quantity of things to do, the car was unloaded and the tents were up by around noon, and the group elected to sit down for lunch: turkey sandwiches.

"So we were talking on the way here," Hunter said, his mouth full of sandwich, "Me and the guys would like to find a spot and go roughin' it for a few days."

"On a trail," his mom, Grace, inquired.

"Well, not ON the trail, but, like, close to one." he responded.

"You know there are bears here," His dad said.

"Yea, but I have bear spray," Hunter retorted.

"And we'd stick together," Austin added, trying to help persuade them.

"And it would only be for two days," Hunter continued, trying to spin the decision in his favor, "a day to get however far we can get and a day to come back."

"So long as you carry the walkies and a compass, I'm fine with it," Hunter's dad agreed.

He got a dirty look from his wife, but she didn't contest his decision. The three friends high fived and thanked them. Then, having finished their sandwiches, ran off to practice ball.

The three played well together and truly loved the sport. Their team had won state last year, though, that was the middle school team. Now, they faced the challenge of making the highschool team.

Though he wouldn't admit it, Hunter was scared for this year. It wasn't just that he would be competing against highschoolers, but it was just the idea of starting high school.

8

He had ruled his middle school. He was class president, and rightly very popular. He had thrived on his quick wit and slightly above average intelligence.

The problem was, he felt there was just nothing spectacular about him. He was a normal kid, from a normal family, with normal grades, and a pretty normal personality. Even though all three friends did manage to make the highschool team, he didn't think what he had would be enough to thrive the way he did at his old school.

Trying not to think about the upcoming school practices, Hunter picked up his bat. He was best at pitching and would have rather practiced that, but Brady insisted that he needed to practice what he was weakest at.

Brady took his spot a distance from Hunter and rolled the ball over in his hand as he prepared to pitch. Austin stood behind Hunter and prepared to catch the ball in the event of a strike.

Brady and Hunter locked eyes, each concentrated on beating the other. Brady secured his footing and pulled back his arm. Then, with as much power and precision as he could produce, he flung the ball toward Hunter.

Tracking the ball as it came in, he swung the bat expecting to hear the crack of the ball hitting the metal. Nothing.

He turned and saw Austin holding the ball in his gloved hand. "That's one for Brady," Austin commented.

Hunter said nothing. His pride wouldn't let him loose. Austin threw the ball back to Brady, and when he had caught it, they took their positions again.

Again, he missed.

Brady smiled. Hunter knew he had been practicing his pitching lately. He was surprised at how much he had improved. However, in the name of competition, he held back his compliment for after the results of the next throw.

9

The ball was thrown back. Brady had lost his poker face and was now grinning, clearly proud of himself. He had never been able to get Hunter to miss twice. Hunter replied with a light, congratulatory smirk and a nod, but nothing more.

Again, Brady steadied himself, drew back his arm, and threw the ball. Hunter had been analyzing his friend's new throw and thought he had it figured out. Tweaking his technique slightly, he swung as the ball reached him.

There it was - that beautiful *CRACK!*

It was a perfect hit. The ball sailed through the air and landed in the open field in the middle of the campsites.

"I'm just him," Hunter joked, spreading his hands and lightly dropping his bat.

"Now that's slang I haven't heard in years!" Hunter's dad spoke up. He had been watching. "I have taught you well!"

Hunter's dad always used dated slang from when he was a kid. Understandably, some of it had rubbed off on Hunter.

"I think you should teach him a little less well," Brady said.

Hunter had learned how to play from his dad. His dad was one of few people he couldn't beat, but that fact itself he owed to his dad. Jack had played ball his whole life and had even played professionally for a few years. He was the one who started Hunter in it when he was younger.

"Well, how about we do something you might can beat him at," Jack suggested, "I was just about to go fishing with Grace and Trent."

Everyone agreed to the idea. After retrieving the ball, and accidentally starting a game of catch, they grabbed the poles and tackle and headed for the lake on the opposite end of the campground.

Hunter didn't mind fishing. He didn't consider himself to be bad at it (though he would never consider himself to be bad at anything). He was, however, often out-fished. He just didn't really have the patience for it if they weren't biting.

Thankfully, today they were. The group caught all the fish they could hope for. Cast after cast they reeled in trout. Some were big enough they elected to keep them for dinner.

Though it was thrilling, the setting sun put an end to their fun. As the evening reds and oranges grew more vivid in the sky, the trout bite began to fade. Satisfied with their haul, the family returned to their campsite.

Each person had kept their two biggest catches. Hunter's mom and Trent rummaged through the endless supplies and arranged a plethora of spices. While they organized the table, Hunter and Brady cleaned the fish: scaling, gutting, and rinsing them. Meanwhile, Austin and Hunter's dad started a fire in the firepit next to the picnic table.

Right about the time when the last rays of light faded, everyone finished. The group converged on the dinner table, filling their aluminum foil wrapped fish with the spices they liked most, then throwing the little packs on the fire.

By now, the flickering red and yellow flames, an electric lantern on the table, and the waxing moon were the only sources of light at the campsite. The group sat around the table and made small talk.

"I say we head out at first light," suggested Austin.

"That's what I was thinking," Hunter agreed, "I wanna get as far as we can before it gets dark."

"And where are you boys thinking you want to go?" Grace asked, a bit of unease in her voice.

"Well, I kind of just wanted to hike up to the top of that mountain there," Hunter pointed through the darkness to a part of the range surrounding the valley, "then just follow the ridge line however far we can get. Try to take in all the views."

"I was kind of hoping to find another lake," Austin spoke up.

"And do that too then," Hunter added, almost liking this idea better than his own.

"I think it sounds fun!" Jack said, breaking the suspense of the mistrusting glare from wife. "Just some guys and nature, the way God intended it."

"I'm not sure that's the way God intended it," Grace shook her head, "You boys better be safe."

"We will Mom"
"Yes, Mrs. Grace"
"Of course!"

"Of course they will! Dinner's ready," Jack announced.

Everyone got up and walked over to the fire. There was a pair of tongs which they used to place the aluminum packets containing the fish onto paper plates. Once they had their meal, they walked back to the table.

Before everyone was even seated, they began to dig in. The meal was largely silent, for no other reason than the amazing taste of the fish. They had been on this type of outing enough to know exactly how to season the fish to perfection - each one tailored to their own taste buds.

Once the food was gone, conversations of planning the week resumed. Then, light conversations about high school started: who was taking what classes, what did they have together, who they liked the best on the baseball team.

Trent retired long before the rest out of sheer boredom. Then, wanting to get an early start, Hunter and his friends joined him around 10:00 pm.

They all entered the tent and positioned their sleeping bags in the most comfortable spots they could find. Once this task was complete, they stopped their chatting, said their good nights, and went to sleep.

Everyone but Hunter anyway. He wanted to fall asleep, but it seemed every way he turned he positioned a lump in an annoying spot. First, there was a lump under his hip; then, when he moved, he found a new one under his shoulder, then under his knee. Finally, he rolled over on his back and stared at the roof of the tent.

The white light of the moon could be seen shining through the translucent nylon, though, it just looked like a blurred smudge by the time it made it through. It was mostly quiet. Crickets chirped, and under that he could hear his parents talking at the picnic table.

Having nothing better to do he tried to make out their words.

"I just don't feel good about it, Jack," his mom complained.

"Honey, he knows what he's doing. All of them do. They'll be fine," his dad's reply became more somber. "This is their last week before highschool. Let 'em be kids before the world forces them to grow up."

"It's not that I don't trust them," his mom countered, "I know they can take care of themselves. He's done more dangerous things before."

"Then what are you worried about?" his dad inquired.

"I don't know. It's just a feeling. Mother's intuition."

"Babe, it's hard for me too," his dad consoled.

"What?" his mom sounded confused.

"Well, he's growing up. Starting high school," his dad explained, "He doesn't need us as much anymore."

"That's not what it is," his mom protested, "I don't think it is... Well, maybe you're right."

"Trust me babe, they'll leave tomorrow and be back Wednesday," his dad encouraged her, "Probably really late Wednesday if I know those boys. And we have the walkie talkies."

13

"Okay. Okay. You're right. It's nothing," she gave in.

Hunter didn't know why his mom got so torn up about these things. He considered himself to be quite the outdoorsman. Plus, he had everything he could need in his backpack. What could go wrong?

With that thought in his mind, he ran over every possibility for tomorrow's journey. What incredible adventures could be ahead. Fighting off bears. Finding food. Blazing a new trail and finding their way back. It sounded perfect. Of course, nothing ever goes quite the way you imagine it.

Chapter 2

Hunter didn't sleep well that night. He usually didn't mind sleeping on the ground, but this night, sleep was hard to come by. That lump just wouldn't go away. He forced himself to lay there, thinking of every trick to sleep that he could. Nothing worked.

Finally, the birds began to chirp. Outside the tent, he could see the first notes of sunlight beginning to light the valley. Having tried to sleep all he cared to try, he got out of his sleeping bag and tip-toed to the door of the tent. Slowly, he unzipped it and slipped through the opening.

He thought he could at least be getting the backpacks ready for when the rest of the group woke up, so he walked to his mom's SUV. In the trunk he found his survival bag, as well as two other backpacks. In the Jeep, he found the hammocks he had brought along.

He took the three hammocks and packed them in one backpack along with flashlights and rope. The other he packed full of food and tossed in a lighter on top.

Once they were full, he lugged them from the vehicles to the picnic table and sat down. He looked at the mountains surrounding the valley. The sun was peeking over the ridge in the East, casting long shadows across the still, sleepy valley.

He tried hard to decide which trail he wanted to take. The day before he had been sure that he wanted to hike up the mountain, but after a long sleepless night to think about it, he was beginning to change his mind. There was one trail that went North, leaving from the lake they had fished at the day before, and one that went West, to the top of the ridge.

He knew if they went North, they could merge off the trail and follow the creek that fed the lake. This would make navigating simple, but he assumed that the creek would follow the valley and not present as many breathtaking views as the one that went up the mountains.

15

Though, to see the views, they would have a lot tougher of a hike. After a few minutes of weighing the pros and cons, he decided he would suggest following the creek.

Feeling confident his decision would lead to the most adventure, Hunter headed back to his tent to wake his friends.

"Brady, c'mon"

"Ugh, what time is it?"

"Time to go. Austin! Austin!"

"Bro, go back to sleep,"

Their less than enthusiastic responses didn't get Hunter down. He knew they would be excited once they got going.

"Come on! The sooner we head out, the further we can get."

Reluctantly, Brady rolled out of bed while Austin drifted back off to sleep. He got dressed, and then the two finally managed to get Austin up.

The three of them then exited the tent and walked toward the picnic table where their backpacks sat ready to go. Hunter's dad was now sitting at the table. He stood up as the three approached.

"Getting an early start I see," Jack commented.

"Not willingly," Austin joked.

"Aww, it's good for you," Jack replied, "Now, which way are you boys wandering off in?"

"I was thinking we could follow the creek," Hunter said as he took the backpacks from the table and passed them out, "If that's okay with you guys."

"I'm good with anything," Brady replied.

"I think that's a wise decision," Jack agreed, "Since that's what your plan is, I want you to keep the creek in sight at all times. Don't wander off course. If you do get turned around, just contact me on the walkie."

Jack reached behind him and picked up a communicator from off the bench of the picnic table. He handed it to Hunter. "Don't lose this. I'll be checking in every so often."

"Yes sir," Hunter complied. He opened his backpack's main compartment and shoved it inside, then zipped it up. He swung it over his shoulder and turned to his friends, "You guys ready?"

Both of his friends smiled. "Yes," they answered simultaneously.

"I want you boys back before the sun sets tomorrow." Jack commanded.

"Yes sir," Hunter said.

"Brady," Brady made eye contact with Jack, "You keep those two in line."

"I will," he agreed.

"Alright, then," Jack smiled and waved his hands forward, "Off you go."

The three boys gave each other excited looks as they began to walk off toward the lake. Now that it was actually happening, Hunter couldn't believe his parents were letting them do this. Sure, they weren't as strict as most, but he wasn't usually allowed to go off on his own like this. This fact made him feel like a real adult. And to be doing it with his best friends made him feel even better.

For the first hour or so, the boys talked and cut up as they walked along the trail, first by the lake, then past that, by the creek. The creek sat in a narrow valley with steep sides. It was shallow, but wide, flowing smoothly over the pebble covered creekbed. Here and there, a rock would protrude from the bottom, stirring the otherwise glasslike surface.

17

Evergreen trees towered over them on both sides of the trail, mostly blocking out the sunlight which was already made scarce by the mountains. Small wild flowers bloomed in the flourishing underbrush. The air was clean and fresh, but also mixed with the cents of the summer foliage. A cool damp breeze lifted up from the creek, putting a bit of a crispness in the summer air.

It was about 9:00 am when the boys reached a spot where the trail turned and went up the mountainside. The creek continued to follow the valley.

"Well, looks like this is where we turn off," Hunter smiled, envisioning the uncharted territory ahead.

"Let's just make sure we don't get away from the creek," Brady chimed in.

"You scared, Skotty?" Austin asked, using the nickname they used for Brady on the ball team.

"No, just cautious," Brady said, "People have gotten lost here before."

"Well, we don't have to worry about that," Hunter said encouragingly, "Like Dad said, we'll keep the creek in sight."

That satisfied Brady and they veered off the trail and into the woods. Already, the terrain was different. The ground wasn't tamed and trampled like the ground on the trail. This only added to the adventure of course.

The boys took turns jumping from rock to rock in the creek, seeing who could stay dry. It wasn't long before each of them had lost their balance and fallen in. Still, each one of them pressed on, allowing the air to dry their clothes before starting another game and falling in again.

Finally, the sun reached its peak. The light filtered through the trees and reflected off of the water as the boys pushed ever toward their unknown destination.

The three talked, occasionally finding a lizard or frog or something else interesting to look at before continuing their journey. Their conversation shifted from wildlife, to life, to school, to government conspiracy theories floating around social media.

"Yea, I heard that the leader of Hungary got assassinated yesterday," Brady said.

"Is that a country?" Austin asked.

"Yea, somewhere in Europe," Brady continued, "That's like the third one this year."

"I saw that too! I think it's just a coincidence though," Hunter said.

"How though?" Brady asked defensively, "When's the last time you heard of someone being assassinated before now?"

"Well, never," Hunter admitted, "I just think if it was coordinated, somebody would already be at war."

"Well, there are wars," Brady added, "Just not in Europe."

"I just don't know if I buy into all of this 'it's the end of the world' stuff," Austin commented over his shoulder.

"That's exactly what people think just before the world ends!" Hunter exclaimed jokingly.

"Well, this just sounds an awful lot about what the Bible says about the end of the world," Brady said.

"You really believe that book says how it all ends?" Hunter asked, genuinely curious about his faith, "Like, they knew that all those years ago?"

"Well, yea," Brady answered, "But, God was the one who knew. Then, He told people to write it all down."

"Just seems kind of superstitious to me," Austin said.

"It would only be superstitious if it was fake," Brady rebutted, "I know it's real. I hope I can convince you one day."

"You can try, Skotty," Austin challenged.

Something caught Hunter's attention that prompted him to quiet their conversation. "Guys, listen."

The two looked forward to Hunter, who was leading the group. Through the noises of the forest, birds, the creek, and the wind, he heard a faint rushing noise up ahead. "Does that sound like a waterfall?"

Brady and Austin listened in, "I guess there's a way to find out," Brady said.

"Investigate!" Austin exclaimed with animated body language, pointing forward.

The three pressed forward. As they did, the rushing turned into a roaring before, finally, their suspicions were confirmed. They came through the trees to an open space. In it was a waterfall, about fifteen feet tall and very wide. From it rushed cascading billows of water; the boys estimated thousands of gallons. Below it was a deep reservoir spanning about fifty feet in every direction, before continuing into the creek they had been following.

The water was crystal clear. Though it was likely about twenty feet deep, the bottom of the tiny lake was in view as if there was no water even there.

For a moment, the boys looked on in awe. "This is better than any view we could have gotten up on the mountain!" Hunter thought.

His gaze was interrupted with a loud splash. Hunter looked in the direction it had come from. Austin was in the water, about twenty feet away. A tall slanted rock lay on the bank beside him and on it was Austin's backpack.

"Oh!" Austin shrieked as he tread water, "That's cold! I mean... Jump on in guys... It feels great."

Hunter smiled and looked at Brady who also grinned. The two then raced over to the rock and tossed their backpacks aside. Hunter climbed up on the rock first, Brady close behind him.

"You sure that's deep enough?" Brady asked just as Hunter was about to jump in.

Knowing it had to be at least ten feet and seeing that Austin had already been successful, Hunter put his arm around Brady and peered over the edge, "Oh, I don't know…"

Without warning, Hunter put his other arm around Brady and pushed off of the ledge. Brady managed to let out a bit of a startled "Oh," Before reaching the water.

The frigid mountain water engulfed the two of them. Initially, Hunter's body was in shock from the cold. However, he quickly gained his senses, and allowed himself to actually enjoy it.

The two boys surfaced, never even reaching the bottom. From there the tree began to horseplay, splashing and pulling each other under the water. When they got tired of that, they took turns jumping off of the rock, then got brave enough to jump off of the waterfall where the ledge was higher and the water was deeper.

"Hey guys," Hunter called from the top, looking down on Brady and Austin below the waterfall, "Rate my dive!"

Hunter took a moment to secure his footing, then pulled his arms over his lead, and dove off the top. He quickly splashed into the reservoir below. Embracing his explorer spirit, he opened his eyes and propelled himself to the bottom to look around.

His vision was mostly blurry so he had to feel around. He could see in one direction a dark spot. Not the edge of the lake, but rather like a continuation of it into a dark area. Though he was a bit disoriented from the dive, it appeared as though the lakebottom continued behind the waterfall. He swam toward the darkness.

The water here was a bit colder, but that was the only change he noticed. The water had become dingy from him stirring it up. He was so focused, he had hardly noticed that he was running out of air. The realization didn't take long though.

Forced to the surface, Hunter pushed off the bottom and began to swim up. Though he felt the water moving past him, it didn't feel like he was making progress moving upward. The light of the sun didn't come back into view.

He began to thrash a bit, trying to swim faster and just as the first notes of panic began to set in, Hunter surfaced. Though, he wasn't where he was before. The roar of the waterfall had disappeared as had the other sounds of the forest. They were replaced with an echoing drip and darkness.

Chapter 3

Confused, Hunter wiped the water from his eyes and looked around. It was hard to see. The only light was coming from below him illuminating a cave cycling and a passageway that extended as far as he could see.

His face beamed with excitement! This was more than he could have ever hoped to find. Not wanting to waste a second, Hunter took a deep breath and dove back down. Rather than following the darkness like he did on the way in, he followed the sunlight to get out. This was much easier.

He quickly resurfaced on the other side, accidentally coming up beneath the waterfall. The water beat vigorously on his head, and he choked as he attempted to take a breath. He coughed as he swam out into the open water. He wiped his eyes and expelled the last of the water from his lungs.

"Hunter!" Brady called, hurriedly swimming over to him, "What happened?"

Austin surfaced behind Hunter near the waterfall. He also rushed over, "Hey, where'd you go?"

He hadn't realized he had been gone that long. However, even just a few minutes without surfacing was enough to send his friends into a panic.

"Did you get stuck or something?" Brady asked.

"No, better!" Hunter exclaimed, though his voice was a bit weak from strangeling, "There's a cave behind the waterfall!"

"What?" Austin asked. He was just now reaching Hunter and Brady.

"There's a cave." Hunter reiterated, "There's a passageway below the waterfall. I found it when I dove off. Come on!"

Hunter began to swim back toward the waterfall. He was too excited to talk any longer.

"Wait!" Brady called.

"How do you get to it?" Austin asked.

"Just swim toward the dark spot!" Hunter called back.

With that, he dove down again, quickly finding the passageway. He realized now that it was quite large, coming up almost to the surface and stretching to the bottom of the lake. It was also wide enough that he could swim in without touching the edges.

He swam through and when the light from the entrance was a ways behind him, he surfaced, once again wiping the water from his eyes.

The cave ceiling was tall. On it hung dangling stalactites from which water dripped into the reservoir of water in the cave. The dip-dropping echoed through air as did the splashing of his every move. Water caustics danced on the ceiling, created by the sunlight shining in below him.

The cave, as well as the body of water in it, stretched back as far as he could see. Running alongside the water, was a ledge, just big enough to walk on. Hunter swam over and climbed out of the water.

He sat down on the ledge and let his feet dangle in the water as he waited for his friends to surface. It wasn't longer than a few seconds before Austin popped up.

He let out his air sharply, then inhaled deeply. "Wow!" he breathed, wiping his eyes and looking around the cavern.

"Right!" Hunter said.

Austin swam over. "Where's Brady?" Hunter asked.

"He swam back to the shore to get the survival bag," Austin answered, "I think he wanted the flashlights."

24

"Oh, yea, that's a good idea," Hunter agreed.

Austin climbed up next to Hunter and sat down in the same position. They admired the cave for a moment, regaining their strength from all the swimming.

"How far back do you think that goes?" Austin asked, pointing into the darkness.

"I don't know!" Hunter said, raising his voice intentionally. The sound verberated around them, feeling as though it shook the walls. The words echoed down the cavern and hung in the air for a long time.

"Pretty far," Austin said, answering his own question.

Hunter and Austin took turns yelling, seeing whose could last the longest. There wasn't time to determine a winner before Brady finally popped up.

He spewed water from his mouth and coughed. "Somebody take this," he choked, lifting a backpack from the water.

Hunter slipped into the water, swam over, and took it from him. Then, they swam over to the bank together. Austin reached down and picked up the backpack, taking it from Hunter, then took Brady's hand and pulled him up out of the water. Hunter climbed out beside him.

Once Brady was on dry ground, he leaned back, panting. "That…was a tough swim," he said between breaths.

"What'd you bring the whole bag for anyway? We just needed the flashlights." Austin critiqued.

Brady sat up and cut his eyes at Austin, "The bag's waterproof. The flashlights aren't."

"Oh," Austin scrunched his face.

"Well, let's get 'em out!" Hunter said, barely able to contain his excitement.

He stood and picked up the backpack, opening it as he did. He rummaged through the contents and pulled out three flashlights then dispersed them among his friends. Brady took his and gained his footing.

They all three switched them on. The light illuminated the passage in front of them. It continued for a long ways and turned left a few hundred feet ahead. The water continued with it as did the ledge beside the water.

The walls and ceiling maintained a uniform proportion, not showing any signs of narrowing or ending. Hunter's face lit up with excitement (if it could get any brighter). "This could go on forever!" he exclaimed.

"Let's go check it out!" Austin said in excited agreement.

"We just need to make sure we don't get lost," Brady cautioned.

"We'll scratch the wall as we go," Austin suggested, pulling a pocket knife from his jeans.

"That'll make it dull," Hunter said, as he began walking forward. He didn't want to waste any time. They would have to leave this place tomorrow.

"It'll be worth it," Austin said, "I can sharpen it again later."

"If you say so," Hunter said, now being followed by the other two.

They walked on. Every so often, Hunter would hear the scraping of the knife on the wall, only slightly audible over the echoing of their footsteps and water dripping from the roof of the cave.

They reached the bend only to find that the cave continued even further into the mountain and turned again. The deep, wide, slow moving body of water beside the group began to narrow into a rapidly flowing creek. The echoing of the flowing water filled the stagnant air of the cave.

With each turn and bend the water grew louder and moved faster. The cave never branched off though. If it had, that would have likely been enough for Brady to encourage the group to head back. The fact that Brady didn't seem worried, made him sure they were in no danger. Even if they were, his exploration would have taken precedent.

"We must be deep in the mountain by now," Brady said over the rushing water.

"Think of all that weight over us," Hunter said.

"I'd rather not," Brady replied.

They walked on for a moment, then Brady spoke again, calling from a ways behind Hunter, "Hey, guys. Look at this!"

Hunter and Austin turned around. Brady was a few feet behind them, staring at the wall.

"What is it?" Austin asked.

"Just come look!" Brady replied vaguely.

Hunter wanted to continue pressing on, but whatever Brady had found had clearly captured his attention. Hunter went to investigate, Austin following behind him.

"Look," Brady reiterated, pointing at the wall.

Hunter looked. Lodged in the solid rock of the wall was a fossilized skull of some sort. It was hard to tell what it was. The only part visible was the tip of its snout. It had large nostrils and sharp, jagged teeth.

"Is that a dinosaur?" Austin asked, beating Hunter to the question.

"I don't know," Brady said.

Brady loved nature and science - especially dinosaurs. Hunter expected him to have some sort of answer. "Come on man, you're the expert."

"I just can't see enough of it," he replied.

"Well, let's see if we can find some more!" Hunter suggested enthusiastically.

They backed up as far as they could without standing in the underground creek, then shined their lights on the cave walls. This illuminated a plethora of shiny fossils lodged in stone walls.

"Wow"
"Cool!"

Brady's eyes grew wide and his face lit up. Hunter knew that, for him, this was better than finding a buried treasure.

The fossils ranged from shells, to teeth, to femur bones. Each one had a darker and shinier tone than the muted tan rock they were embedded in.

"Austin," Brady said, "Hand me your knife."

He did as he said and Brady got to work chiseling into the cave wall near a tooth, about the size of a key. It wasn't long before he had dislodged it from the rock.

"Gotta take a souvenir," he said.

"Let's see how much further back this goes," Hunter suggested, "Then we can come back for some more."

"I don't think we'll have to do that," Austin said from a few feet away.

He had walked down the cave a bit more shining his light as he went. Now that he was looking for it, Hunter noticed that the entire cave was made of the rock holding the fossils. They just hadn't been paying enough attention to the walls to notice.

"This must be like a graveyard or something," Hunter said.

"The whole Earth is a graveyard for fossils," Brady corrected.

This new knowledge in mind, they walked on, their focus less on the path ahead and more on the wall of the cave. They saw thousands of bones and teeth as they walked, but nothing in one piece from what they could tell.

Through all the twists and turns, the cave never split from its path. There were no branching passage ways, just this one tall hallway. Until it stopped.

It wasn't long before the boys reached a wall. The water of the creek rushed under it through a small opening, just big enough for the water to bubble through.

"Oh man," Hunter said, throwing up his arms. His adventure had seemingly run out of mystery, now that the whole cave was explored.

"Well, now we know how far back it goes," Austin commented as Brady inspected the walls closer.

Hunter hung his head back in disappointment. He knew he should have still been thrilled, but something childish in him wanted there to be some sort of undiscovered relic or formation or treasure at the end of their journey. All they got was a wall.

He stared at the ceiling. It too was filled with fossils, mostly shells. But there was something else. A faint dancing light on the ceiling. It almost looked like a reflection of something, but it was more similar to the light created at the cave entrance by the light shining through the water.

"Guys, turn off your lights," Hunter commanded.

"You're not gonna scare us that easily," Brady said.

Hunter hadn't thought of that. It was actually a good idea, but not the point right now.

"I'm not trying to scare you," Hunter eased, "Just do it."

29

Austin switched his off and reluctantly, Brady did the same. Hunter was the last to turn his off. The cave was utterly dark. Hunter couldn't even see the ground he was standing on. But on the ceiling, a faint light shimmered. He looked down to where the water entered the wall. Gently shining through from the other side was sunlight.

"Look" Hunter said pointing (not realizing his friends couldn't see him).

"Look where?" Austin asked.

"At the water," Hunter clarified.

Brady must have seen it because he said, "You're not thinking about trying to go through there are you?"

"Why not?" Hunter proposed, "There's light on the other side. That means once I'm through I could surface."

"If you don't get stuck," Brady countered, "The water's moving and that's a small hole. And even if you make it through, how are you getting back to this side?"

Hunter felt confident that he could fit, but he hadn't thought about getting back through. The water wasn't moving that fast, but it was moving fast enough that it could be difficult to fight.

"There should be rope in that bag," Hunter brainstormed, "We can tie it around that stalagmite," he turned his flashlight on and pointed it to a rock formation a few feet away, "Then, we can use it to pull ourselves back through if we need it."

Brady's face scrunched up. It was his look for "That could work but I don't like it".

"Let's do it!" Austin said.

"I think we should just enjoy what we've already found." Brady said, "Why push our luck and risk getting hurt?"

"We'll be fine," Hunter proclaimed as he pulled the rope from his backpack.

"Famous last words," Brady grumbled.

Hunter ignored him and tied the rope around the rock protruding from the cave floor. He handed his flashlight to Austin. Then, holding the rope, Hunter eased himself into the freezing cave water. It was about waste deep. As he got settled, Brady came up behind him and took the rope from Hunter.

"If you're gonna do something dangerous, at least do it right," he said.

Brady walked over to the stalactite and undid Hunter's knot. He then retied the knot to look much better than the one Hunter had tied. Then, he knotted the rope in a few places for hand holds. When he was done, he handed it back to Hunter, "Thanks, Skotty," he said.

"For the record, this is a bad idea," Brady said.

"See you on the other side," Hunter said, purposely ignoring Brady. It wasn't because he was trying to be rude or dismissive. In reality, he was a bit nervous and trying to talk himself up.

"Don't die!" Austin called.

Brady turned and scowled at him.

"I'll be fine," Hunter said again, seeing the need to comfort both Brady and himself. He couldn't back out now. There were too many exciting things waiting for him on the other side of that wall. He could feel it.

Chapter 4

"I'll tug once if it's safe for you guys to come through and twice if I need you to pull me out," Hunter said.

With that, he turned from his friends, secured his grip on the rope, and slipped under the surface, letting his feet float in front of him. (He wanted to go foot first so that he could crawl back out the way he came if the passage became too narrow to fit.) He then began to slide through a narrow passageway, just barely big enough for him to fit through.

He shimmied along, with the water moving him forward. He shimmied for a few seconds, but realized that the passage wasn't opening up. A bit of unease began to set in. He shimmied faster.

He could lift his head up and see the light ahead of him, but it was impossible to make out how far away it was. The passage narrowed a bit more until it was touching both of his shoulders. He knew he was running out of breath. He tried his hardest to move faster.

Then, his foot became tangled in the rope. He couldn't move forward anymore, but he knew he didn't have enough breath to go back. He raised up and tried to reach his foot, but the passage was too narrow for him to bend down to it. He tried to jerk his foot free from the rope, but it only signaled his friends to pull the rope back.

The tension freed his foot. Now in full panic, he raced for the exit. He clawed his way down the rocky hole. The light began to grow brighter. His lungs commanded that he breath. Finally, the darkness of the cave above him gave way to a blinding light.

Hunter jolted up, flailed his arms, and burst through the surface of the water. He took a sharp, deep inhale before losing his footing and falling back below the gently flowing water. This time, now that his lungs were full, he took a bit more time to secure his footing, and then popped back up again. He stood for a moment to catch his breath.

As he panted, his eyes began to adjust to the light and his brain began to focus on things other than panic and survival like "Where am I?"

When both his eyes and brain finally had adjusted and decided to work together, he noticed that he was overlooking a forest. The creek that he was standing in gave way to a towering waterfall a few yards in front of him. On the other side of that was a lush forest. From where he was, he was looking down at the tops of the trees, nearly level with the tallest ones.

Surrounding the forest were tall cliffs that created a bowl. It was when he noticed the cliffs that Hunter's breath left him once again. This time, not because of panic, but because of awe and wonder. He noticed he wasn't yet out of the cave. Those cliffs towered up into walls and then into a rocky dome covering the whole thing.

At the top of the dome, right at its apex, was a blinding light, but not the sun. In fact, Hunter didn't know what it was. It was bright, certainly not a spotlight, or for that matter, it wasn't like anything he had ever seen or heard of. It was simply a ball of light.

Not sure where to focus his bewilderment, he looked back out at the forest. As he examined the odd landscape closer, he noticed that there was a break in the trees near the middle of the forest, directly under the odd light. The trees mostly blocked his view, but just over the tops of the canopy he could see the tip of a gray stone structure.

Hunter stood there for a while, forgetting that anything existed besides what he was looking at. *THIS* was the reward for his adventure he had been seeking.

Suddenly, Hunter was startled from his gazing by vigorous splashing, gasping, and coughing coming from behind him. He turned to see what the commotion was and remembered then that he had friends.

Hunter rushed over and took hold of his friend, helping him secure his footing. When he finally stopped flailing, Hunter realized that it was Brady.

"Breathe," Hunter prompted him, holding both of his shoulders.

"Oh! Thank God!" Brady coughed, "You're alive."

He took a moment to wipe his eyes and catch his breath. As soon as he did, his eyebrows narrowed, "You jerk!" Brady yelled, pushing Hunter away, "I told you this was a bad idea. I thought for sure you had drowned, and I almost did too trying to save you."

Hunter felt bad. He knew he had given him a scare and Austin was still probably scared on the other side. He hung his head and put one hand back on Brady's shoulder, "Yea, you're right," he admitted, "It *was* kinda stupid but... look around."

Brady cut his eyes up at Hunter, then slowly began to look around. Gradually, his anger faded into amazement. "Woa," Brady breathed, "This is incredible... that was still dumb, but...wow."

"So maybe it was worth it?" Hunter urged.

Brady smiled, "Don't push it."

The two got lost in the landscape and again, Hunter was startled by vigorous splashing coming from behind him. The two turned around to see Austin.

He steadied himself without help and upon seeing the two of his friends standing there safe said, "Oh, good, we're all alive."

"Or all dead," Hunter said jokingly, then directed Austin's attention as he had Brady's.

They all stood there for a moment longer, then climbed out onto the shore where they admired the scenery a bit longer and speculated on what the light source was.

Austin proposed that it was a tiny sun. Brady said that that would be impossible and suggested that it was sunlight, somehow refracted from the surface. It was so bright that it was hard to look at, making determining its source nearly impossible for the friends. Though, Hunter wasn't interested in speculation.

"Why don't we just climb down there to whatever that thing is in the clearing," he suggested.

"Because we don't know what time it is," Brady pointed out, "And we have to be back by sunset tomorrow."

"Why don't we just paige Dad and see if we can have another day?" Hunter countered, "Then we can spend a whole day down here. Plus, if the light is just refracted from the surface, that means it's still daylight outside. We haven't been in here that long."

Hunter could tell that curiosity was even getting the best of Brady, "Fine," Brady said, "We'll see what your dad says. Austin, grab that walkie talkie outta the bag."

"You mean the bag back on the other side?" Austin said.

"You left it?" Brady complained.

"I thought the two of you were stuck!" he defended, "You think I was worried about grabbing the bag?"

"Well, if you put it that way…" Brady said.

"I'll just swim back and get it," Hunter suggested.

"You wanna go back through there and come back again?" Brady questioned, "I barely even want to go back through to get out of here."

If Hunter was honest, he didn't really want to do that again either. Still, more than not wanting to retrieve the backpack, he longed to explore the cave further, "It was just the shock of doing it the first time," Hunter hoped, "It'll be easier now."

Reluctantly, he slid back into the water and made for the opening. He held his breath, quieted his mind, and forced himself back through the opening.

To his surprise, it was actually easier. He pulled himself along using the knotted handholds Brady had tied in the rope and quickly surfaced back in the cave.

He fumbled in the darkness until he found the backpack. He closed it up and, now having more confidence to go through the opening, slipped under the water, tugging the bag behind him.

With little struggle he surfaced back on the side with his friends. "See," Hunter said once he had his breath, "Much easier."

He waded over to his friends and tossed the bag over to Brady who took out the walkie while Hunter climbed out of the water. Brady fidgeted with the buttons for a while, but said nothing.

"What's wrong," Hunter asked, seeing that Brady's face was uncertain.

"There's no signal in here," he explained.

"Guess you went back through for nothin'" Austin said.

Hunter thought for a moment. This couldn't be the end. There was something amazing, even more amazing than what they had seen so far, and it was right through the trees. He couldn't leave. Not yet.

"Come on guys," Hunter stood up.

"Hunter," Brady said, "We can't go down there. We'll run out of time. And what if your parents have been trying to contact us for the last hour?"

"Dad's not one to panic," Hunter said, "He'll give us until he said we have to be back before he comes looking for us."

"I don't know…" Brady said, "That's an awful lot of worry to put them through."

"I think I agree with him for once," Austin sighed.

Hunter wasn't ready to let this go yet, "Come on guys. Even if they get mad at us, even if we're late, we are standing in the middle of a groundbreaking discovery! Subterranean life!"

"Then why don't we leave it at that and come back later," Brady interrupted.

"Let me finish," Hunter urged, "Not only that, we're standing on the verge of high school," he grew a bit more solemn, "I know we say nothing could split us up, but let's be real, that's not how high school works. We're gonna get busy and get girlfriends and then eventually go to college. This is our last chance to just be us, together. Our last chance to be kids before the world makes us grow up."

His friends stared at him for a long while. Brady was deep in though, and Austin was waiting to hear what Brady said. "Well..." he started. The other two boys leaned in, "I guess if we make it quick, we could be back here in an hour and out half an hour after that."

Hunter smiled. "But we have to make it quick," Brady reiterated.

"We'll be lightning fast," Hunter promised.

"Well, let's get a move on it," Brady said, standing up and walking past Hunter toward the edge of the waterfall.

Austin stood up and walked past Hunter next, "Your speech was beautiful," he teased, though still with sincerity.

"Thank you," Hunter said, taking a bow and then pushing Austin forward.

Hunter picked up the backpack with their supplies, swung it over his shoulder, and followed behind them. At the edge of the cliff was the waterfall. It was more narrow than the one outside the cave and less water flowed over it. However, it was much taller, about thirty feet from top to bottom.

Going down beside the waterfall were giant fallen rocks, made mossy by the spray from the waterfall. They were just the right size and positioned in just the right way so that the group could easily go down them. And, when the time came, they could also easily go back up.

When they all had reached the edge, Hunter took his place back at the front of the group and began his descent. The waterfall cascaded down beside him. A cool mist blew from the falling water, but since he was already so wet, it didn't make much of a difference to him.

It did however make a difference on the rocks. The moss and water made them slick. "Be careful on these rocks," Hunter called back up to his friends.

He reached the bottom, and as he did, Austin began making his way down. While he waited, Hunter took a moment to examine things from his new vantage point.

The water from the waterfall created a small pool like the one on the surface that had led them here. The water from the pool narrowed on one end and flowed into the forest and out of sight.

He was only now noticing that the air here wasn't like the cold stagnant air of the rest of the cave. It was hot and steamy. The air was thick. It reminded him of when he and his family went to the Caribbean on vacation one time. It felt tropical.

It didn't take long for Austin to reach the bottom and Brady quickly followed. "Let's get going, Lightning," Brady taunted.

"Eye, eye, Captain" Hunter soluted.

The group trudged through the thick underbrush toward the center of the cavern. They found that the creek flowed toward the structure. This was good because the underbrush was so thik, walking through it would have been impossible in some places. The creek created the only open space to walk through. It was becoming evident that this wasn't a forest, it was a jungle.

Once they were under the canopy of the trees, it was easy to forget that they were in a cave at all. The light broke through the leaves just like the sun would and the marbled gray ceiling of the cave mimicked a partly cloudy sky.

"You know what's weird," Brady said.

"Other than being in an underground forest?" Austin said.

"Yea, other than that," Brady conceded.

"What?" Hunter asked.

"There are birds chirping," He replied.

Hunter hadn't even noticed it as out of place. The birdsong fit right into the landscape and had seemingly evaded detection by his brain.

"What's weird about that?" Austin asked.

"Well, it looks like this place is completely shut off, except for the way we got in here," Brady replied, "Unless there's an opening we haven't seen, somebody would have had to bring the birds here."

"I guess we can't be the first ones to find this place," Hunter said, both trying to rationalize the facts and find out where Brady's mind was going.

"I guess," Brady agreed, "Especially if this stone structure we are walking to is man made, but why bring birds? It's like they were trying to replicate another place. And on that thought," He promptly added, "Where did they get these plants? None of these plants grow anywhere around here. They look tropical."

It was all a bit odd. A bit of unease was beginning to break through Hunter's determination for adventure. What if there were people here, or traps, or dangerous animals?

"We should be getting close," Hunter said, trying to change the subject. Surely there was nothing to be afraid of. There hadn't been anyone here for years, if they had been here at all.

As if to answer his comment, the clearing came into view ahead of them. What Hunter saw, he could hardly believe. "Oh, wow!" He exclaimed, speeding up and breaking out through the treeline.

Before him was a massive pyramid. It was made of layers upon layers of thick gray stone, each layer making a square, and then a smaller square on top of that one. Running up each of the four flat sides of the pyramid was a staircase, laid on top of the already existing stair stepping layers of the pyramid. At the top was a cubic structure with an opening on each side which each of the four staircases lead to. The creek they were wading through split and flowed in a circle around the pyramid, creating a barrier between the open grass and the thick jungle.

"No way," Brady said from behind Hunter.

"Wahoo!" Hunter yelled, his excitement getting the better of him. He ran up to the base of the pyramid and began springing up the stairs to the top.

"Wait!" Brady called out, "You don't know…"

"Come on Brady!" Hunter called back, "Booby traps aren't a real thing. Get up here!"

Austin answered by running past Brady toward the pyramid. Then, rolling his eyes and putting his better judgment aside, Brady gave into his excitement as well and began running up the pyramid stairs.

Seeing his friends were both on the way, Hunter focused his excitement back on his discovery and continued racing toward the top.

About half way up, he turned back and called to his friends, "Come on slo…" he stopped mid sentence.

Something caught his attention. More than his attention - it caught his whole mind. Hunter put his hand on his head and closed his eyes. What was this feeling?

It was like he was experiencing something so familiar, like he had experienced it a thousand times, yet he had never experienced it before. A slight tingling sensation ran through his body.

With that sinsation, glowing green lines shot down the stairway, illuminating them with a thick, almost tangible, green light. The light pulsated and moved in a sort of electrical pattern - like the pattern of a lightning bolt as it cuts through the sky, but spread out over the entire stairway.

"What's going on?" Austin called out.

"Get off the temple!" Brady yelled as he grabbed Austin and ran back down the stairs.

Hunter wanted to listen, but he couldn't. He wanted to run, but he had to continue his journey to the top. Every fiber of his being was scared, yet at the same time, sure of what he needed to do. Coming from the top of the pyramid was a call. A beckoning call that filled every corner of his mind and forced him upward.

"Hunter!" Brady yelled from the bottom. He ignored him and continued upward.

The closer he got to the top, the fainter the voice of his friend, and the voice of his own mind became, as both were consumed by the call. Finally, he reached the cube at the top of the Pyramid.

Coming from the cube, was a bright green glow, the origin of both the green lights under his feet, and the call. Inside the cube was a white, metal obelisk about four feet tall. It was meticulously crafted with flowering, swirling patterns. On top of the obelisk was the light. From the light, the green lightning cascaded down the obelisk and onto the ground where it was directed to the stairs which Hunter now noticed were metal: the same metal as the obelisk.

He looked into the light from which the call was coming. His heart pounded with excitement, but Hunter didn't know for what. Nearly beyond his control, he raised his hand and reached for the light.

As his hand got closer, the light dimmed revealing a small green crystal floating above the obelisk. It called to him. He took hold of it.

The moment his hand closed around the crystal, the green energy raced up his arm and across the rest of his body. In that same instant, a massive blast of energy erupted from Hunter's closed hand. The blast ripped through the cubed structure he was standing under and sent pieces of stone flying in every direction.

The energy intensified around Hunter's body, engulfing him in a bright green glow. A searing heat began to run throughout his veins. He wailed in pain.

Again, a blast of energy came from Hunter. This time, it wasn't just his hand, but his entire body that released the energy. The blast radiated through the cavern, but mostly directed itself upward where it met with the cave's ceiling and the mysterious light illuminating the cavern.

The two energies mixed. The white light became mingled with the green energy. Its stable, unwavering consistency became unstable, wobbling and shooting off bolts of energy that jared rock loose from the ceiling. The rock crashed to the ground. Finally, the sphere lost all stability and exploded, sending a shockwave through the cavern. The entire cave shook and a hole was punched through the roof revealing actual daylight.

With this larger blast released, the green radiation disappeared from around Hunter's body. The burning sensation was gone as was the deafening call of the crystal. With these stresses gone, Hunter's mind began to slip out of consciousness. His eyes grew heavy and he felt himself begin to fall before drifting off into darkness.

Chapter 5

Hunter slowly began to wake up. He was totally disoriented. His eyes opened to a blur of colors, nothing quite in focus. For a moment, he felt a pain in the back of his head, but it quickly subsided. With the disappearance of the pain, came the refocusing of his vision.

He was looking at the sky. What he at first thought were clouds, were actually the remnants of the cave ceiling that still towered over him. Within the gray rock directly above him was a gaping hole revealing the sky above, lit with the colors of the setting sun.

He lay there for a moment, still getting his bearings. As he did, he heard the patterning of footsteps and Brady's voice calling his name. Hunter turned his head to the side and saw his friends running up the stairs.

Trying to prove he was okay (though he wasn't yet sure if he was) Hunter sat up just as Brady and Austin reached him.

"Are you okay?" Brady asked, kneeling down next to Hunter.

"I think so," Hunter answered honestly. He didn't feel any pain in his body. By now, he actually felt quite normal.

"Can you stand up?" Brady asked, Austin looking anxiously over his shoulder.

"Yea," Hunter tested out his legs, "Yea, I think so."

Brady motioned for Austin to help and they each took an arm, helping their friend to his feet. He actually found that he didn't need help. Everything was just fine, and now, he was confident in that fact. Whatever happened, hadn't affected him physically.

"I'm good, guys," Hunter said, pulling from their helpful grip and standing on his own.

"Are you sure?" Brady asked.

"Yes." Hunter confirmed.

"Then, what were you thinking?" Brady questioned.

"I was…" Hunter recalled the overwhelming urge he'd had to take hold of the crystal. He didn't want to sound crazy, so he deflected, "I didn't think it looked dangerous."

"You didn't think the glowing green thing in the ancient temple in an underground forest looked dangerous?" Brady questioned with a loving, yet condescending tone, "You could have gotten killed."

"Yea, maybe not that smart in retrospect," Hunter agreed.

"Well, at least you're okay," Brady said, "Is your 'need for adventure' finally satisfied?"

"More than satisfied," Hunter breathed, now ready to leave. This experience had been unsettling for him.

"Well then let's get outta here," Austin said, finally speaking.

It was only when they turned to walk away that Hunter noticed he was still gripping something in his hand. He pulled it up to inspect as the other two boys started down the stairs. He turned over his hand and opened it. Still there was the small green crystal.

It glowed softly now, just enough for him to still be able to tell that it was glowing. He must have been looking at it for too long because Brady turned back to see why Hunter wasn't following. His eyes fixed on the crystal.

"You're not taking that with us are you?" he questioned from a few steps below Hunter.

"Why not?" Hunter replied, "It doesn't seem dangerous anymore."

"Did you see what just happened?" Brady asked.

"I think that had more to do with the obelisk," Hunter answered, turning to gesture to it. When he did, he realized that it was gone. It

44

looked as though it had retracted into the pyramid. All that was left was a metal over on the ground where it had once been.

"I don't know," Brady said.

"Well, I can't put it back now," Hunter pointed out.

"Just please be careful with it," Brady conceded, "I want us all to make it out of here alive.

Hunter agreed and placed it in the backpack on Brady's back. Then, they made their way down the stairs, headed for the exit. When they reached the bottom, Hunter took one last look at the pyramid.

He felt a mix of emotions toward it. The first was pride. As most boys do, he had always dreamed of finding something like this, but he'd never thought that he actually would. The next was shame. The cube that had once been at the top was completely blown to pieces. The light that had shone above it was gone. He couldn't help but feel he had ruined this strange place. Then, the final and lasting emotion came - unease. This was all so strange and out of place. An underground world, totally different from the one above. An out of place ancient temple. On top of all of that, the strange things that had just happened, the way he could hardly controle himself, the crystal, the explosions. As he turned away from the temple, he was actually quite glad to do so.

The friends trudged back through the forest and up the small creek. The cave was much dimmer without the strange light. Now the only light came from the hole above them, and the sun was setting quickly.

"I could use a flashlight," Austin said from the front of the group.

"Yea, me too," Hunter said from the back. He reached ahead of him to Brady, opened the backpack, and dug for the flashlights. As he did, a voice came from the walkie talkie.

"Boys, come in Boys," it was Hunter's dad, "Is anyone there."

The hole in the cave ceiling must have allowed the radio to regain a signal. Hunter took it out and held it to his mouth.

45

"Yea, Dad. We're here."

"I was beginning to wonder if you were ever going to pick up," He said, not scolding, but stating it in a way that asked where they had been.

"Oh, we're only now just hearing you. Maybe the mountains are blocking the signal." Even though Hunter knew good and well what was blocking the signal, he didn't count his statement as a lie. More as a misdirect.

"Well, I'm glad I got a hold of you. Now your mom will go to sleep tonight." He chuckled, "If you haven't made camp, it's probably about time to do that."

"Yea, We'll make camp soon," Hunter promised.

"Alright then," he said, "You boys sleep tight. I can't wait to hear all about it tomorrow."

"Heh… Yeah… Can't wait to tell you," Hunter said, only now realizing that he may not want to share the details of the trip. For one thing, his parents would not be happy with some of the risks that they taken to get here, but also, how could they believe such an outlandish story?

Hunter placed the walkie back in the backpack and continued looking for the flashlights. He rummaged until he found them, and then passed them out.

"So how are we gonna explain all of this?" Austin asked the group.

"I say we just tell them," Brady suggested.

"I'm not sure Mom will ever let us out of her sight again if she finds out how we got in here," Hunter pointed out, "Pluss, how could they even believe us?"

"Well, for proof, we have that green crystally thing with us," Brady said, "As for them believing us, we could just bring your dad here and show him. Then, he can see who we need to report it to."

Hunter did like the idea of reporting what they had found. He imagined the headlines "TEENS FIND ANCIENT UNDERGROUND RUINS". He didn't even mind telling his parents about it. What he did worry about was the fact that these ruins seemed to have some sort of strange properties.

"What if this place needs to stay a secret?" Hunter thought out loud.

"What do you mean?" Brady asked.

"Well, there's clearly some sort of ancient advanced technology here. The light, the obelisk, the lights that started when I touched the crystal. If movies have taught me anything, it's that the government doesn't like that kind of stuff to get out."

He left out the part about his mysterious draw to the crystal. Not only was it harder to explain, it felt eerily more spiritual than the other things they had seen. Plus, he didn't want to sound crazy.

"Those are just movies," Austin chipped in.

"I agree with him," Brady said, "We have to report this. And there's a giant hole in the ceiling. Someone will report this place eventually. Might as well be us."

"Unless we mysteriously disappear after we report it," Hunter grumbled.

Their conversation for now was cut short as the beams of their flashlights struck the falling water of the waterfall. The last rays of sunlight were gone and their flashlights were all that illuminated the cave.

Carefully, they climbed back up the slick rocks to the top of the bluff overlooking the underground oasis. It was dark, but as they reached the top, the moon came into perfect alignment with the hole above them. The moon was waxing and shone brightly in the clear night sky. The soft white light illuminated the cavern, accentuating the leafy tops of the jungle below.

47

Hunter had quickly made it to the top of the bluff, but he noticed that his friends were tiring out. Both of them shivered. Hunter had noticed the drop in temperature, but it hadn't affected him near as much. He wanted to press on and make it out of the cave tonight, but he decided to suggest something else.

"How about we make camp here for the night?" He asked.

"In here?" Brady questioned.

"Sure," Hunter affirmed, "We're all tired and cold, and since we made it from camp to here in a day, we can make it back so long as we head out early."

"That sounds good to me," Austin said, clearly exhausted.

"Well," Brady thought for a moment, "I guess it would be best if we were well rested before we hiked back through the cave."

"Perfect!" Hunter said, "Let's get out the sleeping bags."

"You mean the ones back at camp?" Brady said.

The realization took a moment to reach Hunter. He had only prepared hammocks because he expected that they would be in the woods and even those were on the other side of the cave.

Hunter sucked air through his gritted teeth, "Well," He couldn't think of any sort of plan other than sleeping on the rocky ground.

"Well is right," Austin said as he sat down.

Hunter felt bad. He hated that he hadn't planned better. But how could he have known they would spend so much time here or even find something like this place?

"Honestly," Brady said, looking around, "I'm so tired, I could just sleep on the ground."

"Me too!" Austin agreed. He had already leaned back against a boulder nearby.

Hunter wasn't sure that he was tired enough to find the ground comfortable, but as long as his friends were satisfied with it, he could make do.

It didn't take long for the three to find spots to lay down. Brady took a spot beside Austin on the same boulder. It leaned back at a reclined angle, and didn't look that uncomfortable. However, there was just enough room for the two of them, so Hunter chose a spot a few feet away.

The spot he chose was on bare dirt. He laid back and pulled his hands up behind his head, raising him up just enough to look through the hole into the night sky. The moon had partially moved away from the opening so that now only half of it was visible.

As he lay there thinking, he realized that he hadn't slept since the trip had started. Of course, he had tried the night before, but was unsuccessful. He realized that his body wasn't exhausted. He should have been from the activities of the day, but it felt as though he could have walked back to camp right then. What was tired was his mind.

The event at the pyramid had really strained him. He still couldn't make sense of it. Had his curiosity just gotten the better of him? No. No, that couldn't be right. He was drawn to it. Like it was calling him. Wasn't he? Yes. Maybe. Yes.

But that's crazy. Was he going crazy? No. Something had actually called him. Something had forcefully drawn him to the crystal. But what? How would that even work? Technology? Witchcraft? No. That's not real. Is it?

Hunter's mind eventually became so full that he could focus on the questions no more. He tried his best to shut them out and watch the moon move across the opening above. Before it was completely out of sight, Hunter had drifted off to sleep.

Chapter 6

Hunter's eyes jolted open. He wasn't sure what had woken him, but whatever it was had startled him.

He raised up and looked at Austin and Brady. Both were fast asleep against the rock. The moon had now moved away from the hole above, making the cavern much darker. He couldn't tell much about the forest below, but all seemed calm and quiet. The only exception was the light pattering of the waterfall and the bubbling creek that fed it.

Had he heard something? Was it a bad dream? Hunter didn't know. He wanted to go back to sleep, but was very thirsty. He only now realized that he hadn't had anything to drink since the night before. His survival skills told him not to drink from the creek, but his thirst said otherwise. He decided that a few sips wouldn't hurt.

He stood to his feet. It was nearly impossible to see the ground before him. Not wanting to accidentally fall in the water, Hunter sluggishly stumbled over to Brady. He felt around until he found the backpack beside him and took from it a flashlight. Turning it on, he walked to the edge of the water.

Before kneeling down, he shined the light around the area, looking for whatever had woken him. He wondered if there might be an animal nearby. He didn't see anything, so he proceeded to get a drink.

He cupped his hands and scooped them through the water, then drew them to his mouth. The cool water absorbed into his dry tongue. When he swallowed, he could feel the water travel down to his stomach, refreshing him.

He wanted more, but decided to stop after a few handfuls. His dad had always taught him that water, no matter how clear, could have contaminates. He didn't want to push his luck.

Feeling better now, Hunter raised up, intending to walk back to his spot and lie down. However, before he turned around, he heard what sounded like footsteps. He froze.

Fear began to rise up within him. Was there someone here? A bear? Whatever it was, Hunter wanted to be ready to act as soon as he turned around. He listened.

Again, he heard footsteps. They sounded bipedal. Human. Maybe there was an ancient protector for the temple that he had accidentally blown up.

He shifted the flashlight in his hand and gripped it firmly, ready to use it as a weapon. The steps were growing closer, now directly behind him. His anxiety rose. Building up all of the courage he had, he spun around.

When he did, the beam of the flashlight revealed a human just a few feet away. Acting purely on instinct, Hunter swung the flashlight at the figure as hard as he could. The swing narrowly missed. Almost mid swing, Hunter realized the figure was Brady.

"Woa!" Brady cried, jumping back.

"Brady!?" Hunter exclaimed both relieved and annoyed, "What are you doing?"

"Seeing what you were doing!" he retorted.

"By sneaking up on me?"

"I didn't mean to!" Brady insisted, "I didn't know you were that on edge."

"We're in a cave with a temple and an underground rainforest!" Hunter replied, "Of course I'm on edge."

"I'm sorry," Brady apologized.

With the adrenaline subsiding, Hunter became more grounded, "No, it's not your fault," he replied, "I must have had a bad dream or something. I thought someone else was…"

Like before with the crystal, something stopped Hunter's train of thought. Following his instincts, he looked over Brady's shoulder.

51

Standing over Austin was the shadowy silhouette of a man. In his left hand was Hunter's backpack, in his right was a pistol.

Within just a fraction of a second, the man raised the gun, firing at an oblivious Austin. From the barrel came a yellow flash of light. The light rapidly dispersed over Austin's body and faded.

With the same motion, the man pivoted and pointed the gun in Brady and Hunter's direction.

"Get down!" Hunter yelled, throwing Brady to one side and diving to the other. A yellow bolt of light passed between them.

The second Hunter hit the ground, he scrambled to his feet. Already the man was firing, this time at Brady. Brady still had no idea what was going on, and before either of them could react, a yellow blast had reached Brady. The light spread across him and his body went limp.

"No!" Hunter yelled, not knowing if his friends were alive or dead.

With his exclamation, came more blasts, this time aimed at him. With the man's gun pointed at him, it was as though everything slowed down. He could tell exactly where each blast of light would land, and moved out of its way.

Through a series of frantic ducking, weaving, and finally rolling to the ground, Hunter dodged each blast. After the aggressor had fired a few shots, they stood there looking at one another.

"So you do bear a crystal," the man said.

"I don't know what you're talking about," Hunter snapped.

The man lowered his gun, as though he were about to say something else. It was then that Hunter saw his chance. Seeing no other way of escape and not caring what the man had to say, he charged at the attacker.

As he ran, the man attempted to move aside. However, he couldn't move fast enough. Hunter rammed into the man, throwing him against the same rock that Austin's motionless body was propped against.

Only when his head smashed into the rock did Hunter notice that the man was wearing a helmet. Still, it was hard to make out any details in the darkness.

Realizing he had a chance, Hunter raised his fist to punch the man. With adrenaline fueled courage, he thrust his fist toward the man's head.

Not showing any signs of being caught off guard, the man ducked out of the way. Hunter's hand made contact with the rock, but instead of breaking his hand, Hunter broke the rock. The impact of his punch caused the boulder to crack and a significant chunk to fly off.

For what had to be only a few microseconds, Hunter's mind paused in surprise. This was just enough for the attacker to scoot away and use some sort of rod to sweep his feet out from under him.

Hunter's back met the floor of the cave with great force, knocking the wind from him. Almost before he reached the ground, the man was already on top of him, holding the rod to Hunter's neck. Hunter grabbed hold of the rod with both hands and pushed, trying to save himself from being strangled.

"Hold still," the man commanded, his voice transmitted through a speaker in his helmet.

"Get off me!" Hunter choked, becoming more and more panicked.

"I don't want to hurt you!" the man insisted.

"Tell that to my friends!" Hunter gritted his teeth.

With that statement, a warm, familiar sensation began to fill Hunter's body. He felt his grip tighten and the force of the rod on his neck begin to fade. A green glow filled the air.

Hunter was so focused that he hardly noticed any of this until a flowing green pattern appeared on his hands and arms. The same

53

green cascades of energy that had been flowing over the pyramid earlier were flowing over his body.

Hunter was utterly confused, but saw an opportunity. He tested his strength by lifting the rod off his neck a bit. Then, confident in his ability, yanked the rod to the side and flipped the man off of him.

The man hit the ground with a thud and Hunter rolled on top of him in the same fashion the man had done to him. It wasn't long before he had the rod pressed against the man's neck.

"What are you?" Hunter commanded.

The man moved his head a bit and his helmet retracted, "I'm just like you," he said.

Hunter scowled at the man, "What do you want? What did you do to my friends?"

"I just stunned them," the man said calmly, "They'll be fine. I didn't know you were a crystal bearer. I thought you boys had just found it. I was just going to take it and leave."

Hunter had a hard time believing his story. Why would he show up now, just hours after they had?

"You just discovered your powers didn't you?" the man asked.

Hunter only looked at him through the green glow of the energy flowing across his body.

"I bear a crystal as well," the man was smiling now, "Let me help you."

Hunter was intrigued now, but wasn't sure if he could trust him. "Prove that my friends are okay first."

"Of course," the man agreed, "Can I stand up?"

Hunter answered by getting off of the man, but holding the rod at him. The man then stood up. Without Hunter having to ask, the man unclipped his utility belt and laid it, and the strange gadgets attached to it, on the ground.

"May I?" the man asked, pointing to Austin who was only a few feet away.

Hunter lightly gestured the rod in that direction and circled around the man to allow him to pass. Once the man had reached Austin, he knelt down.

"Look," the man said, pulling at Austin's shirt then lifting it up, "No burn marks or redness," he then let go of the shirt and placed his index finger on Austin's neck, "And his pulse is quite strong. You can feel it if you like."

The man's actions were beginning to convince Hunter that, at the very least, the man didn't mean them harm. Hunter's green energy began to fade from his body as his adrenaline subsided.

"No, I believe you," Hunter said. He thought for a moment, weighing his options and thinking of his next question. He wanted to know what this man knew about this energy, the crystal, why he was here. Before he could settle on one, the man spoke.

"My name's Daniel," he said, "Daniel Sons."

"I'm Hunter," Hunter said, not seeing the harm in giving up that information.

The man stood up. Hunter pointed the rod at the man who held out his hands in a surrendering gesture.

"I came here because our sensors picked up an anomaly," the man explained, "A massive burst of cosmic radiation, not matching that of our solar system."

"Who do you work for?" Hunter asked, "The government?"

"I work for myself," Daniel said, "It's kind of a long story."

"I've got time," Hunter insisted.

"Not enough," Daniel retorted.

"Answer my question," Hunter demanded.

"Well, I guess I can give you the short version," the man agreed, "Over the past few hundred years, a secret organization has worked to secretly destabilize the world and its many governments. They use crystals like yours to power their armies, armed with technologies you couldn't even dream of.

Not many years ago, I discovered that organization and have worked to fight against it ever since then. Which, of course, includes collecting those crystals before they do."

"How many crystals are out there?" Hunter demanded.

"Well, that I can't be sure of," Daniel said, "I know of eight, yours being the eighth. They are hard to track down because they don't exactly stand out unless your nearby or they release a lot of energy like yours did today."

"So why hasn't this organization shown up yet?" Hunter inquired.

"By the grace of God," Daniel said, a bit flamboyantly, "They will though. Soon."

Hunter thought for a moment. His logic said that the man was lying. This story was absurd. However, his instincts told him that he was telling the truth. Since they had been right so far, he decided to trust his instincts. He stopped pointing the rod at Daniel and held it vertically, resting one end on the ground.

"Is this organization going to kill me?" Hunter asked, seeing the logical end scenario.

"If they find you, they will likely take you with them to study you," Daniel admitted, "They don't often come across those who can wield a crystal."

This didn't sit well with Hunter. He had seen too many movies like this and none of them turned out good for the lab rat. His brain worked to try and comprehend what he was hearing. Could this even really be true?

"You know," Daniel continued, "I have a base where I could protect you."

Hunter gave him a distrusting glare.

"If you'll come with me, I can hide you from them," he continued, "You'll be safe, and, when you learn to control your powers, you can help me fight them."

Hunter tightened his grip on the staff, "I'm not going anywhere with you," he insisted, "For all I know you want to experiment on me too."

The man shook his head, "I've known you for five minutes and already I can tell that you're so much like my son," The man rubbed his face. Hunter only glared at him.

"I won't force you to go with me," Daniel said, "But at least let me offer you something."

"I'm listening," Hunter said.

"You keep my gear," Daniel offered, "This suit that I'm wearing has an AI built into it. You can use him like a training program. Here,"

The man reached to his chest and grabbed a circular device from above his sternum. Once he had taken hold of it, a white light began to spread across his body, and the dark material he was wearing turned into a black cloud. The cloud swirled around and was absorbed into the disk in Daniel's hand, leaving behind tight fitting, black underclothes.

"ALI," Daniel said.

"Huh?" Hunter questioned, thinking he had misheard him.

"Yes sir!" A voice called from the disk.

Hunter had no idea what was going on.

"Back up your memory to the jetpack I'm carrying," Daniel requested. Hunter peered around Daniel, only now seeing the slim, silvery backpack Danile was wearing. "Once you've done that, upload a copy of your base programming to this puck and transfer ownership to Hunter... What's your last name?" Daniel looked up at Hunter.

"Oh, um... Hogan," Hunter answered, quite confused.

"Hunter Hogan," Daniel continued, "Be sure and upload a copy of the training program that I made for Dylan."

"Of course sir," the voice said from the disk, "It will take me a moment."

"Take your time," Daniel replied.

"Who is that?" Hunter asked.

"Dylan?"

"Well, him too, but I was talking about the voice coming from the disk," Hunter corrected.

"Oh, the voice in the puck, or disk as you're calling it, is ALI," Daniel explained, "He's an AI that I invented to help me. Now, I'm making a copy of him to help you."

"Oh," Hunter said, his brain still processing everything that was happening.

"And Dylan, well..." The man paused sentimentally, "Dylan is my son," he looked at the ground.

"It's okay that you don't trust me," Daniel said, almost as if to answer Hunter's thoughts, "I haven't even given my own son many good reasons to trust me, so I wouldn't expect you to. Whether you do or not, you can trust me when I say this," he looked into Hunter's eyes, "I'm going to do everything that I can to protect you, kid. I'm just not sure if everything I can do is going to be enough."

"What do you mean?" Hunter asked.

"The Organization will come for you once they find out you have a crystal."

"Then take it," Hunter said, "I don't want it that bad!"

Daniel looked past Hunter at the backpack, then back at Hunter. "They'll come for you even if I take it. It's safer if it stays with you," Daniel insisted, "I'll do my best to redirect The Organization, but you have to keep all of this a secret," he paused, "from *everybody*."

"Well, two other people already know," Hunter informed, looking between his two friends (who were still unconscious).

"They didn't see enough to be able to remember anything from before they were stunned," Daniel said, "It will be as though they slept through the whole night to them. When they wake up, you can't tell them. You can't tell your parents. You can't tell anyone. You especially can't use them in public. Anywhere that there's a camera, you're just a normal kid. In fact, you avoid cameras, that includes sports, if you play them. You break either of these rules and, I promise, they will find you."

The cold remarks were heavy. How was Hunter supposed to keep this kind of thing a secret? He had superpowers! Something like that anyway. And no sports? No baseball? This was crazy.

"What?" Hunter exclaimed, "I can't do that!"

"The alternative is that you come with me," Daniel said bluntly, "Or, well, I guess the other option is that you go with The Organization."

"How do I know you're even telling the truth?" Hunter said.

"You know," Daniel said, void of any emotion. He sat the puck down on the ground and pressed a button on a wrist watch that Hunter only now noticed. "Like it or not, this life chose you. It's up to you what you do with it."

Daniel turned away. A small flame appeared at the base of the shiny, rounded piece of metal he wore on his back.

"Where are you going," Hunter asked.

"Back to my base," Daniel said smiling, "I'm expecting my son soon. I'm sure I'll see you around. The crystals have a way of bringing us crystal bearers together."

"But..." Hunter didn't know what he wanted to say. It felt like there was so much more to know. How could he just give up everything based on this? Everything he believed to be true was being uprooted by the words of a mysterious stranger.

"You might want to put your friend back where he was," Daniel said, turning back and pointing to Brady, who lay motionless next to the creek.

Before Hunter could say another word, Daniel leaped from the edge of the bluff. He dipped just below the cliff before shooting back up, the jetpack carrying him into the distance.

As he flew toward the hole in the ceiling, a U shaped aircraft appeared, hovering in the opening. Hunter could just make out a wave from Daniel as he landed on top of the ship and climbed inside. As soon as he was out of sight, the aircraft sped off, quickly disappearing from view.

Hunter could only look on in shock, amazement, confusion, and a myriad of other emotions. He stared at the hole for a while with only one thought echoing in his mind "What am I going to do?"

Chapter 7

Hunter leaned back against the remnant of the rock he had broken earlier and pressed his hand to his forehead. "Literally, what just happened?" he asked himself out loud.

Was this even real? This whole thing was absurd. The underground ecosystem, he could maybe believe. The strange crystal, he could maybe believe. Even the mysterious visitor, he could maybe believe. But all of this, all at once, and somehow being able to glow. It just felt like some twisted dream.

Then, there was the story of the man, Daniel. To say he was a spy or something and that the world was about to end, there was just no way that it was true... Was there?

"It would seem you are in distress," a voice said, startling Hunter. He flinched and the green glow spread across his body, startling him further.

"My apologies," the voice said, "I didn't mean to scare you."

Hunter looked at the rippling patterns of green light on his hands and arms, then looked for the source of the voice. The green glow coming from his body illuminated something in front of him.

It was like a hologram, but more solid looking. It was completely black and appeared to be made of small particles or dust, almost like a black mist. It formed a ball, not solid, but separated into lined sections. Under the mist was the "puck" that Daniel had given him.

"Allow me to introduce myself," the strange emblem moved as a voice was projected from it, "I am ALI, an Artificially Living Intelligence. It would seem that I have been duplicated and assigned to help you navigate your new abilities."

Hunter stared at the AI. He was stuck in a strange gap of being both overwhelmed and curious.

"You are Hunter I presume," the voice asked.

"Yea," Hunter replied. The energy around his chest and arms faded involuntarily, allowing for darkness to surround him.

Hunter didn't like not being able to see the thing in front of him. He didn't trust it. He focused hard to try and make his energy come back. He shook his arm and tensed his muscles, but nothing worked.

"You haven't yet mastered connecting with your powers," ALI said.

"It would seem that way," Hunter conceded, frustrated.

"I can help you with that," the AI offered.

"And how is that?" Hunter asked half heartedly, giving into the overwhelmed side of himself and slumping down into a crouched position against the boulder. A sleeping Austin propped up beside him.

"Your powers are connected to your subconscious," he said, "You must connect with them there."

"Oh, now I understand!" Hunter exclaimed sarcastically, "Thanks for clearing that one up."

Hunter's mind didn't know where to focus. He felt so powerless and defeated. Not because of his powers not coming to him. He couldn't care less about that. He felt defeated because he simply had no way to comprehend what was happening.

"I know this must be a lot to throw on you at once," the voice said.

"Yea, kind of," Hunter replied.

"The world is a bigger, more complicated mess than you could even imagine," the AI informed in a consoling voice, "You don't have to understand it all at once. But you, as a crystal bearer, have a bigger, more complicated role in cleaning up that mess than the rest of the population."

"No, No I don't," Hunter retorted, "I came here for one last adventure with my friends before High School starts next week. I don't want to fight a war. I just want to go to high school next week and do my best to be popular. How am I supposed to hide these powers and do that?"

"You don't," the voice said, "If you reveal your powers, then you will be forced to fight. If you wish not to fight, then you will be forced to conceal them."

"Why should I even believe any of this?" Hunter asked with frustration.

"Why shouldn't you?" the AI asked.

"Well, for one, it's crazy."

"Therefore it's untrue?" the voice asked, "It's crazy that you glow but that is true. Why should you question the rest of the things you have heard?"

The voice had a point. Hunter knew that his problem was that he didn't want to believe it. If it were all true, then his life was ruined. He pulled up his knees, crossed his arms around them, and placed his head between them.

After a moment of silence, ALI spoke, "Allow me to help you."

"How?" Hunter asked, not looking up.

"Stand up," ALI commended.

Hunter reluctantly did as he said.

"Your powers are neither a burden nor a curse," ALI continued, "They are a gift."

"I don't see…" Hunter was interrupted by ALI.

"Of course you don't, it's dark. You haven't yet seen what you can do. That is why you don't understand. Follow my instructions."

Hunter waited for them. He wasn't sure what was about to happen but he wasn't hopeful that it would change his outlook.

"Take a few deep breaths," ALI instructed.

Hunter obeyed.

ALI continued, "I want you to think of people that you love,"

"I,"

"Do it!"

Hunter rolled his eyes, but conceded. He ran the names of his friends through his head, followed by his family. Nothing happened. He thought of their names again, but still nothing.

"Whatever was supposed to happen isn't happening," Hunter complained.

"Then you're not doing it correctly," ALI contested, "Think of your experiences with those people. Think of why you love them."

Willing to give it one more try, Hunter followed his instructions. He began to think about his friends. He thought about the fun they'd had the day before, exploring and playing. He thought about their times playing ball together and winning state together. The memories were comforting. He thought about Brady's caution and the way he did his best to protect the group. He thought about Austin's boisterousness and love of all things fun.

He also thought about his family. He thought about how he and Trent liked to annoy one another and how Trent was always there when he needed someone to talk to. He thought about the times he had played catch with his dad and how strong he was. He thought about the way his mom always cared for him and how loving she was.

Even in the chaos and questioning, these thoughts caused Hunter to smile. The memories were warm to his confused heart. They were a pleasant distraction that actually served to ground him, halting the swirling storm of emotions that had raged in his mind.

"Now," ALI said, "Keep focusing on those good thoughts and call your powers once again. Think of what you want them to do."

Hunter did as he said. He held his hand out in front of him and imagined the energy flowing over it. A warm sensation filled his heart and began to spread across his body. With the warmth came a green glow.

Starting at his chest, green streams of energy began to flow across his upper body. The streams weren't rigid, yet still composed of straight lines and geometric corners. The patterns traveled down his arms, all the way to his finger tips.

He smiled, "Woa,"

"Very good!" ALI congratulated.

"Okay, this is cool," Hunter admitted, "I'll give you that."

"It's amazing what a new perspective can do for the mind," ALI said.

"I'm still not saying this is the greatest thing ever," Hunter said, "I'm just saying it's cool."

"Well, in any case, would you like to learn how to use them?" ALI asked.

"What can they do?"

"More than I know how to teach you," ALI said, "But I can teach you what I know how to teach you."

"Well, there's no way I'm going back to sleep anyway," Hunter realized.

First, prop your friend back up against the rock," ALI instructed, "Then, climb down the waterfall to the forest."

Hunter agreed, first walking over to Brady. He reached where he lay, only about a foot from the water's edge. He was on his back, laying in the same position that he had fallen in. Like Austin, there was no sign of any burns from the energy blast that had knocked him out.

He looked peaceful, Hunter thought, as he picked him up from his shoulders. He was surprisingly light, or more accurately, Hunter was surprisingly strong.

Hunter drug Brady back to the broken rock and propped him up next to Austin, where he had started the night. When this was done, He walked to the waterfall and climbed, once again, down the slippery boulders. Trailing behind him was the spherical emblem of the AI, formed from the black dust.

He reached the bottom and hopped off of the last boulder, next to the pool of water at the base of the waterfall. He noticed that his natural curiosity and sense for adventure had returned. The anxieties of what this all would mean had momentarily slipped from his mind, and he focused on learning about his powers. It seemed that a giddy joy had risen in Hunter as he realized the dream of every young boy had come true in him - that being the wish for superpowers.

Hunter looked to the orb next to him, barely able to make it out in the darkness. "Well, teach away," Hunter insisted.

"Yes sir," ALI replied, "I must say, I am programmed to train with the blue crystal. The properties of yours could be a bit different. This will likely require a bit of trial and error."

"As long as you know what you're doing," Hunter said, smiling. He held out his hands in front of him and called his powers, reaching out to them easily this time. He admired the glowing green patterns as they once again spread over his chest and arms.

"Lesson one will be summoning your crystal." ALI said, "Open up your hand and stretch it toward the crystal."

Hunter did as he said and listened for his next instructions.

"Close your eyes. Feel its warmth. It calls to you, tells it to come to you. Envision the crystal in your hand."

Hunter once again followed his instructions, creating an image of the crystal in his mind. He could feel the energy within him intensify. He imagined the crystal flying out of the backpack, through the air, over

66

the ledge, and into his open right hand. As he envisioned it, it happened.

The crystal soared through the air and came to rest in his hand. As it made contact with his skin, he felt the energy in his body grow in intensity. He opened his eyes. The green glow spread over his entire body now, illuminating the scenery around him and reflecting off the surface of the water.

"This is so cool!" Hunter exclaimed.

"You have only scratched the surface of your ability," ALI said, "You will be strongest when you are touching the crystal, but you can draw power from it from anywhere."

"Kind of like a quantum battery?" Hunter asked, recalling the main powersource for nearly all modern technology.

"Precisely!" ALI agreed, "In time I'll teach you exactly how the crystal, and you for that matter, work. But let us focus on your instinctual abilities for now."

"Okay…What are those?" Hunter asked, sliding the crystal into his pocket.

"You will see," ALI replied vaguely.

After he spoke, the mist that formed his circular emblem faded, then quickly reformed in a shadowy human-like shape. It stood with its hands in a fighting stance.

"Ummm…What are you doing?" Hunter asked, only slightly concerned.

His slight concern was quickly replaced with shock as the figure pulled back its arm, lunged forward, and swung his fist at Hunter. He sensed it like he had the blasts from Daniel's gun and dodged out of the way. Hunter, now on guard, stared at the figure that stood frozen.

"Very good," ALI said from the figure, "Your senses are like an echo location of sorts. You can sense intentions, objects, and predict movements."

"Yea, I did that when I fought Daniel earlier." Hunter informed ALI.

"Yes, I know," ALI said, "Now, this time, fight back."

The figure unfroze and once again began attacking Hunter. The first few advances, Hunter only moved out of the way. He had never been in a real fight before, unless you count what he had done earlier. He didn't really know how to fight.

After a few more times of this, the figure began to move quicker and more skillfully. It didn't take it long to land a blow on Hunter's chest.

"Ounch!" Hunter wined, stumbling backward.

"Mistakes in battles have consequences," ALI called from the figure, "So will they in these simulations. Fight back!"

The figure attacked again and this time kicked Hunter in the same place on the chest. This thrust him back into one of the boulders he had climbed down on.

"Stop that!" He complained, "I don't know how to fight like that!"

Hunter was now more annoyed that he was curious. The excitement was gone. ALI didn't acknowledge him and the figure walked over to attack again. Out of necessity, Hunter pushed himself off of the rock, out of the way of the figure which punched the rock.

"Seriously ALI! Stop it!" Hunter was angry now.

The figure pivoted to swing at him again, but Hunter dodged. When he did, he returned with his own swing. As his fist flew through the air, the green energy surrounded it and concentrated in front of Hunter's fist.

His punch made contact with the figure. When it did, a green wave of energy, mixed with the figure's black mist and spread out through the air in front of him.

Just when Hunter was about to celebrate, he felt something. Something behind him. He spun around, dodging the attack of another figure created from the black mist.

This time, Hunter didn't hesitate. He called the energy to his fist and punched through the chest of the shadow. The green shockwave filled the air again as the figure was blown apart.

Another one formed behind where the previous figure had stood. Hunter smiled upon seeing it. He was no longer fearful or angry. This was fun.

The new figure ran forward. It thrust its fist at Hunter, but he caught the figure's arm with his left. The texture was odd, a bit squishy like flesh, but cold and rough like sand. It threw him off a bit and the figure used its free arm to swing at him.

Hunter sensed it though and moved out of the way, ducking down yanking the attacker's arm. This pulled it off balance. Hunter saw his opening and punched up through the figure, filling the air with the satisfying wave of green and black.

Hunter pivoted from side to side, looking for the next figure to form. I never did. Rather, ALI's lined orb appeared in front of him.

"Very good!" he congratulated, "Your form is sloppy and your reactions are a bit slow, but some training will sharpen that."

"Thanks?" Hunter said, not sure if that was a compliment or an insult.

"Now let us try another thing," ALI suggested.

"Sure!" Hunter said, once again eager to learn.

"Call your power to your fist, like you are going to punch something."

Hunter did as ALI instructed. The energy flowed from his chest and down his right arm to his fist. A bright concentration formed over his knuckles just as he commanded it.

"Now open your fist and move the concentration to your palm," ALI said.

Hunter once again did as he said. He opened his fist, holding his hand out flat, and focused hard to make the energy concentrate below his palm.

"You might not want to point it that direction," ALI suggested, "Hold your hand out. Point the energy at one of the trees over there."

Hunter adjusted his hand so that his fingers were pointing up and his palm was facing the tree line. "Like this?"

"Precisely!" ALI said, "Now pull as much power from the crystal as you can and focus on the tree in front of you. Envision it forming a beam between you and the tree. Tell the energy what you want it to do."

Hunter stared at the tree, squinting in the near darkness. He Felt the crystal in his pocket and commanded that energy come from it and travel to his palm. It listened.

Hunter's body once again glowed with the green energy. A bright ball formed in front of his palm. When it looked like he had held the charge long enough, he pushed the energy out in a beam.

The green ray of light split through the darkness and slammed into the trunk. The whole tree began to shake. The energy surrounded it and traveled up the trunk and to the branches surrounding it in the same glowing patterns that surrounded Hunter's body.

The ground trembled and there was a subtle groaning noise. Then, the tree began to vibrate. As it did, its trunk began to stretch and expand. It popped and cracked as its branches grew in every direction and began to make for the cave ceiling. The tree, still glowing, was now the tallest tree in the underground forest by at least twenty feet, and its glow illuminated the entire cavern.

"Wow!" Hunter exclaimed as the tree's growth slowed and the vibrating stopped.

"Well, that wasn't at all what I expected to happen," ALI said.

"What were you expecting?" Hunter asked, not taking his eyes off the towering tree.

"Well, the blast should have exploded against the trunk, knocking the tree over," ALI informed, "It would seem you have an ability Daniel has never come into contact with."

"So I can make things grow?" Hunter asked, looking at ALI.

"Give me a moment to analyze your energy's wavelength, and I should be able to tell you exactly what it is you have the ability to do."

ALI's bubble rippled for a moment. For a while Hunter continued to examine the tree. Then, while he waited, he toyed with his powers, making the crystal float out of his pocket and race across the surface of the pool of water. Every once in a while, racing it through the waterfall.

It took ALI about five minutes to speak again.

"I've got it!" ALI exclaimed.

The sudden noise started Hunter and he lost focus, and the crystal dropped into the water. Embarrassed, he promptly summoned it out of the water, to his hand, and placed it back in his pocket.

"So," Hunter said, trying to ignore what just happened, "What did I do to the tree?"

"It would seem that your energy precisely matches the wavelength of Adenosine Triphosphate or ATP, when a phosphorus is detached from the base," ALI said.

"And what is that in English?" Hunter asked.

"All of life on Earth uses ATP for energy. Specifically, they use the energy created by the breaking off of a Phosphate atom from the

Adenosine base. The energy that is released then is identical to the energy of your powers."

"So what did I do to the tree," Hunter asked, not understanding or caring about ATP.

"You gave the tree unlimited energy," ALI replied, "I suppose that since it had a sufficient water and mineral source, its growing potential was as unlimited as your power."

"Oh, now that's cool!," Hunter said, "Let's see how big I can make it!"

"I don't think...," ALI was cut off as the energy once again formed a beam between Hunter and the tree.

The tree groaned and creaked. It began to vibrate. Once again its trunk expanded and the branches reached for the ceiling.

Feeling spry, Hunter raised his free hand and conjured another beam. It tore through the humid air and made contact on the now gargantuan trunk of the tree. The glow of the energy on the tree intensified and filled the Cavern with an almost daytime amount of light.

Just as the branches were nearing the top of the cavern, the growth slowed to a halt. Hunter, confused and wanting to make it all the way, pushed more energy through the tree.

When he did, the three began to sway from side to side. It began to creak and pop. Upon hearing this, Hunter immediately shut off his powers. He looked up at his creation through the once again dark cave.

"Guess I got it a little too tall," Hunter admitted.

"I don't think that's the problem," ALI said, a bit of manufactured uncertainty in his voice.

As Hunter stared at the swaying tops of the tree, he noticed something falling toward him. Lots of somethings, gently drifting through the air. As they reached him, he realized they were leaves, dead, dry leaves.

"What caused that to happen?" Hunter asked, as the leaves continued to rain down all around him.

"I believe you did," ALI said a bit smartly, "You only speed up what the tree would eventually do. It had endless water, endless energy, but there were not endless minerals in the ground to sustain such a thing."

"I killed it?" Hunter asked.

As if the tree wanted to answer the question itself, a horrible creaking echoed through the cave, followed by a loud pop. Then, cracking, and screeching, and more popping.

The tree began to lean in Hunter's direction. His eyes grew wide as saucers. Seeing that the tree was falling toward the cliff, Hunter began to run into the forest.

He trudged through the pile of fallen leaves and swiftly waded through the creek that led to the pyramid. All the while, the popping and cracking grew louder. Eventually, it overpowered the sloshing of the water he was traversing.

Then, finally, CRASH! The mammoth tree made contact with the cliff. The commotion was followed by the sound of falling rocks as they were jared from the bluff.

Once the noises stopped, Hunter did too.

"I would say, yes, you did in fact kill the tree," ALI condoned as his emblem reappeared beside him.

"Oh!," Hunter exclaimed as he came to a horrid realization, "My friends!"

"Are perfectly fine," ALI added calmly.

"How do you know?" Hunter asked, barely staving off pannick.

"I checked on them already."

73

Comfort flooded over Hunter and he hung his head back, finally able to take a breath of relief. A smile spread across his face, and he began to laugh.

"I don't see what's so funny?" ALI questioned.

"That…Was…Awesome!" Hunter yelled, "Did you see that!"

"Unfortunately I did," ALI said confused, "You could have wiped out the whole forest or your friends!"

ALI had a point, but Hunter was too wrapped up in enjoying his new powers to be bothered by "what ifs".

"But I didn't," Hunter remarked, "I'm just realizing, you and Brady would get along really well."

"Well, he must be a very good person then," ALI said, matter-of-factly.

"He is," Hunter agreed, "But that wasn't a compliment."

"Nevertheless, I will take it as such," ALI decided.

"Have it your way."

The two emerged through the tree line on the scene of the crash, ALI's emblem floating next to Hunter. The first tinges of daylight were beginning to illuminate the cavern through the hole in the ceiling.

The tree had clearly crashed into the cliff about three quarters of the way up the side. Where it struck the rock, a chunk was missing. The tree had fallen diagonally, so when it hit, it deflected off the side where it fell into two pieces which now lay on the ground, mingled with large boulders. The roots of the tree had not given way, rather it appeared that the trunk had snapped about twenty feet off the ground.

Hunter surveyed the damage for a moment, then spoke, "So, what else can you teach me?" he asked ALI.

"Quite a lot," ALI said, "But your friends will be waking up soon and you have a secret to keep."

Hunter had been feeling good up until this point. He didn't like the idea of this. The distraction that the training had offered was gone. "I don't think that's necessary," He complained.

"Even still, once a secret is given, you can never take it back," ALI said, "All I ask is that you take a bit of time to learn from me. When I have taught you everything I can teach you, make your decision based on that. You haven't even had your powers for twenty four hours. What if you discover later that you should have kept them a secret."

Hunter thought over ALI's advice for a long moment. He had never been in the business of keeping secrets, and on top of that, he really wanted to show off what he could do. Still, ALI had a point, a good one. Sure, some of these things he had heard tonight could be lies or exaggerations, but it didn't feel that way. Plus, he could at least take some time to figure it out.

"Fine," Hunter agreed, "I'll keep it a secret."

"I think that is a wise decision," ALI agreed, "Now, you must pack up the equipment Daniel gave you before your friends wake up."

Hunter turned to climb up the rocks beside the waterfall, which, thankfully, had not been disrupted by the falling tree. As he did, ALI spoke.

"And maybe don't let them look over the ledge."

Part 2: Darkness
"Though I walk through the valley of the shadow of death"

Chapter 8

Hunter once again scaled the rocks next to the waterfall and made his way back to the makeshift camp at the top. By the time he had completed the climb, daylight had illuminated the cavern. The soft morning rays beamed in through the hole in the cave ceiling and revealed a humid fog that hung in the air.

The gear that the mysterious visitor had left the night before still sat in a pile near his unconscious friends. Among it was the metal rod, now retracted to about a fourth of its full length, a round "puck", as it had been called, and the odd gun that had been used to knock out Brady and Austin.

Hunter spied the red fabric of the survival bag and walked to collect it. He dumped the contents out on the ground and began to place the gear in the bottom, to hide it. As he did, he closely examined each piece, turning it over in his hands.

They were practical in nature. There was clearly no effort to make them look like anything more than hunks of metal. Still, they had a certain fantastical element to them. Their simplicity showcased their advancement. Their creator didn't need to add bells and whistles to make them effective. They were the tools of a soldier.

"So what do these things do anyway?" Hunter asked, calling ALI and placing the items in the backpack.

A small slit opened on the puck and the particulate black mist rose from it. It reformed ALI's emblem a distance away and he spoke, "They have many functions. All of which I will teach you, in time."

"That was an incredible non-answer," Hunter pointed out, looking up from his task.

"There simply isn't enough time to tell you right now," ALI said, "Their applications are vast and your friends will be waking up any minute."

As if to answer him, Brady began to stir. The mist making up ALI's emblem quickly retreated inside the backpack where the puck now was.

Hunter quickly scooped the rest of their supplies back in on top, making sure that the flashlights and walkie were easy to reach. He didn't want anyone digging through the bag and discovering his secret.

Brady yawned and took a deep breath. Hunter stood up, swinging the backpack over his shoulder. "Good morning sleeping beauty," he teased.

"'Morning," Brady replied sluggishly, "What time is it?"

"I don't know, but the sun just came up about an hour ago," Hunter answered, not wanting to get the walkie from the bag.

Brady stood up and rubbed his forehead, "You've been up that long?"

"Yea," Hunter said, "Guess I just couldn't really sleep too good last night."

"Well, I slept like a rock," Brady said, still rubbing his head. He paused for a moment, "I've got a splitting headache though."

Hunter could hardly hide the look of guilt on his face knowing exactly what had caused it, "Oh…um," Hunter put his hand on his neck, "Well, maybe you just need a drink of water."

Brady looked over to the stream, "Out of there?"

"Sure, a little bit won't hurt," Hunter assured him.

Brady agreed and walked over, stooping down to drink. While he did this, Hunter walked over to Austin and shook him, "Come on, Ausin! Time to go."

Austin's head bobbed back and forth a few times before his eyes finally opened. He looked up at Hunter dizzily. "It can't be morning already," Austin complained.

"Yep! And we need to get a move on it if we're going to make it back to camp before dark," Hunter urged. He was trying to get his friends out of this part of the cavern. He didn't want them to see the fallen tree or anything else that might have been out of place.

Austin slowly stood to his feet. He put his hand on his forehead and scrunched his face, "Man, I've got a splitting headache."

"Me too!" Brady said, walking back from the stream.

"Huh," Hunter said, His facial expressions betrayed his culpability, "It must be the air in here. Probably should get out so we can get some fresh air."

"You're probably right," Brady agreed, "Maybe it has to do with whatever is keeping everything in here alive."

"Must be!" Hunter said dismissively, making for the creek.

"Don't you have a headache too?" Austin asked.

"Huh?" Hunter paused with one foot in the water and one on land, "oh, yea, terrible headache," Hunter massaged his forehead and turned back to the creek, stepping off into the chest-deep water.

He waded up to where the water bubbled out of the opening they had used to enter this section of the cave. He pressed his hand against the wall of rock that separated this lost world from the rest of the cavern and followed it down to the slim opening. After fumbling around for a moment, he took hold of the rope they had used to get back and forth. Once he had done this, he looked back to his friends.

Both of them stood on the bank staring at Hunter. He had succeeded in keeping their attention away from the fallen, dead tree, but apparently, had directed too much of their attention to himself.

For a moment he contemplated just giving up and telling them his secret. He didn't really want to keep it anyway. Still, if he could just get them out of this part of the cave, he was sure he could go back to acting normal.

"Well guys, are we leaving or not?" Hunter asked.

Brady and Austin looked at one another and then back at Hunter. Austin cut his eyes back and forth between his two friends, clearly waiting to hear what Brady had to say. Hunter waited in suspense to see if he was going to be successful or not.

Brady narrowed his eyebrows and tilted his head, then spoke, "Yea, we're coming."

Hunter knew that Brady was suspicious; he could hear it in his voice, but he knew he didn't have evidence of anything specific yet. Hunter suspected that he could keep it that way once they were out of this cave.

Brady and Austin entered the creek. "See you on the other side!" Hunter farewelled, diving beneath the surface of the crystal clear water, and pushing the red backpack in front of him. One by one, each boy took hold of the rope, shimmying back through the tight passageway and surfacing in the pitch black darkness of the part of the cave they had entered through.

The sounds of the flowing water and the boys' splashing echoed through the cavern. Hunter swam and tossed the backpack up on the ledge that ran along the side of the underground creek. He fumbled through the bag in the darkness, took a flashlight off the top, then closed the bag. Once he had turned it on, he climbed up onto the ledge and offered each of his friends help getting up.

As soon as everyone was on the ledge, they made for the exit, taking little time to admire the cave as they had done on the way in. It wasn't long before notes of daylight began to shimmer on the ceiling. They had reached the exit.

79

"Well, looks like our little adventure has reached its end," Hunter said, actually feeling a bit sad. He sat down at the water's edge and dangled his feet in the water. Though he had rushed out of the rest of the cave in an attempt to keep his secret, he almost didn't want to exit this final time. There was so much that he would have to figure out on the other side: the world, his powers, his life.

"It's just the end of this adventure," Brady said, sitting down next to Hunter, then sliding off into the water. "There will be plenty more for us later."

"Yea!" Austin agreed, "We've just gotta survive High School first." He slapped Hunter on the back and then cannon-balled into the water.

Hunter smiled at the optimism of his friends. He couldn't help but catch some himself. Maybe he could keep his secret and things still be the same. He didn't have powers before and everything was great. As far as his friends knew, he was the same person he was when he entered that cave. And really, he was the same person. Just stronger, faster, and glowier. Maybe the best thing to do was keep the secret anyway. And if it wasn't he could tell them whenever he wanted.

Those thoughts filling his mind, he too slid off into the water, and together, they dove under the surface. Ahead of them, the sunlight illuminated the round exit like a portal leading them back to the real world. Together, they swam through.

***

The rest of the week went on as you'd expect. The boys surfaced under the waterfall, ending their adventure in the same place it began. They reclaimed the supplies that they had left behind and arrived at their camp just as the sun was setting.

They all agreed not to mention the temple or Hunter's incident. Brady's agreement came reluctantly. However, Hunter had convinced his friends that even if someone else discovered the cave later, they would all know the truth. Who would have believed them anyway? They were just kids.

They spent the rest of their vacation fishing, hiking, and playing ball, allowing their experience in the cave to sink into the back of their minds. The only problem Hunter ever ran into was that his swing and pitch were extremely powerful. Even though he was holding back, the first time he swung at a ball, when the bat made contact, the ball burst into pieces. He was able to blame it on the ball being old, but after that, Hunter made sure he only ever played catcher.

Also during this time, Hunter would sneak off at night to train with ALI. He found that he didn't need more than about three hours of sleep. In fact, he couldn't sleep for longer than that if he wanted to. The training helped him pass the time.

As far as Hunter knew, no one had caught on to his secret, and if he was being honest, he kind of liked it that way. He could just be himself around his friends and family. He didn't know how they would react if they found out, and he liked the way things were.

Of course, he didn't fear that they would reject him or anything like that. He knew they would love him no matter what. He just worried that they would think of him differently in some way afterward. He couldn't place exactly what that way would be though. He simply liked the way things were and didn't want anything to change.

Then, the day came. Not the day to leave the campsite. No. That day came and went. Monday came. Hunter's scariest adventure yet, even for someone with superpowers. Actually, especially for someone with superpowers. The first day of High School had arrived.

***

"Hunter! Are you awake?" Gracie called down the hallway.

Hunter's eyes jolted open, and he sprang from the bed. The cold air chilled his body as he flung off his cocoon of blankets.

"Yea, Mom! I'm up." It wasn't a lie. He was up when he replied.

He had overslept! How could he do this? He didn't even really need that much sleep anymore. Still, he had stayed up too late listening to ALI explain his powers and what he knew about the mysterious organization Daniel had mentioned.

81

He ran into the bathroom that separated his room and Trent's and began frantically brushing his teeth. He only had fifteen minutes before he had to leave.

As he brushed his teeth, he began using his powers to float his various school supplies across the room and into his open backpack. Green energy flowed over the surface of binders, pencils, and notebooks as they paraded across the room. He finished both tasks at the same time and dashed from the bathroom back to his bedroom.

On the nightstand next to his bed sat the puck and the green crystal beside it. Morning sunlight beamed through the window and struck the crystal, reflecting off its surface. The crystal levitated about an inch above the wooden table, spinning slowly on its axis.

On the opposite side of the room was his closet and on the adjacent wall was the door that led to the hallway containing the guest room and Trent's room.

Hunter grabbed his backpack off the floor in front of his bed and zipped the top shut. Then, he tossed it up on the unmade sheets. He used his powers once again and summoned a pair of jeans and a T-shirt across the room and into his hands.

The green energy radiated around them the same way it did his body when he used his powers. As they reached his hands, also surrounded by the green energy, he sensed his dad coming down the hall.

"Son, it's time to go," Jack insisted as he walked toward Hunter's open door.

Hunter conjured a small blast of energy directed at his door. He sent it across the room, slamming the door shut. He knew that wouldn't last long.

He summoned the crystal to his right hand and called the puck to his left, shoving both of them under the covers just as his dad eased the door of his room open.

"What's taking so long?" Jack asked.

"I overslept," Hunter hurriedly replied.

"Well, hurry up," Jack insisted, "You don't wanna be late on your first day."

"Yea, Dad. I know."

Jack walked out of the room, and Hunter quickly got dressed. He then took the puck and the crystal out from under the sheets. As he held the two next to one another, a spot opened up on the puck in the exact shape of the crystal. ALI had done this so Hunter could keep the two together.

He placed the crystal in its spot and then placed them in his backpack. There was a small compartment in the bag just big enough for the puck where he figured no one would find it.

Having done all of this, he threw the pack over his shoulder and rushed down the hallway into the living room.

In the living room there was a curved sectional couch which separated the living room from the dining room. Against the wall opposite the couch was a T.V. The volume had been turned up to blaring levels, as was the custom in the household in the mornings. Gracie liked to listen to the weather forecast as she cooked.

Trent sat on the part of the couch facing away from the T.V. and was finishing a pancake. Hunter's dad was reading the paper at the dining room table, and his mom was cleaning up from cooking breakfast.

"Honey, I made you some pancakes," she said.

Pancakes were Hunter's favorite for breakfast. He could even see that she had gotten out the blueberry syrup. "Alright!" he said excitedly.

"If he's going with me then he's just gonna have to eat one on the go," Trent said as he stood up from the couch.

"Come on, Trent," Hunter complained, "I'll eat quick. Give me five minutes."

"Nope!" He said. He walked over and lifted his backpack from one of the dining room chairs and started for the door.

"Trent!" Hunter whined.

"Trent, wait on your brother," Jack commanded, not looking up from his paper.

"Ugh, fine," Trent conceded, "Make it fast, hotshot. I'll be in the Jeep."

Hunter walked to the counter next to the stove and threw a few pancakes on a paper plate. Behind him was kitchen island. He sat his plate there and drowned the pancakes in syrup. As he scarfed them down, his mother spoke.

"Now honey, you have a good day, and don't worry about anything. I'm sure…"

Hunter listened initially, but the word "UFO" caught his attention as the T.V. played.

"Yea Mom, sure," he brushed off her concern, "Listen to the T.V."

She turned her attention to the T.V. On the screen was a blurry video of something moving quite quickly across the sky. It would have been just another UFO video to anyone else, but Hunter recognized the shape. It was the same shape as the U-shaped aircraft the mysterious visitor, Daniel, had gotten into when he left the cave last week. A woman's voice played over the video.

"Things like this video, taken in Montana, have been reported not just all over the country, but all over the world over the past twenty four hours. One man even claimed to see two figures on jetpacks flying over his farm in rural Nebraska."

A picture flashed across the screen quite clearly showing the outline of two human-like figures a few hundred feet off the ground.

A bit of unease began to rise within Hunter as he remembered the warning given to him by Daniel. If even half of when he and ALI had told Hunter was true, this could be very bad.

"Even right here in Colorado…"

"Alright, Hunter, that's enough of that," his mother said, turning the T.V. off with the remote sitting next to her on the counter.

"But…" Hunter didn't know how to respond. He needed to see the rest of that news cast.

"No buts!" she insisted, "Your brother is waiting on you. Go have a good day!"

He couldn't argue. He slouched away from his empty plate. "Aren't you forgetting something?" Gracie asked from behind him.

"I'm in a hurry!" He teased, knowing exactly what she was talking about, "My brother's waiting on me."

"Get over here!" his mom playfully insisted.

He turned around and gave her a hug. Once he was done with that, he made for the door. "Go conquer the world!" his dad called after him.

"Maybe I should start with conquering high school," Hunter replied as he twisted the door handle.

"Good plan!" Jack agreed, and Hunter slipped out the door.

He walked down the short sidewalk to their carport where Trent sat in the jeep honking the horn.

He smiled because he was truly excited to start high school today. Over the past few days, as he had grown in his abilities, he had begun to look forward to this day. This is because he didn't feel clueless or scared of them anymore. They even made him feel a bit more secure.

Sure it may be a challenge to hide them, and maybe high school would come with its challenges, but he felt like if he could master these powers, he could master high school too.

Still, the news report had left an uneasy feeling within him. Maybe it was your typical UFO sighting, but Hunter couldn't help but think that here was more to it.

Chapter 9

The highschool was only about fifteen minutes away. As Trent drove, he began to tease Hunter.

"You know, most freshmen on the ball team get shoved in the toilet on the first day. It's a kind of initiation."

"And you would know since you're such an athlete," Hunter said sarcastically, taking out his phone to pass the time.

"I'm just sayin' that I've heard rumors," Trent insinuated.

"Well, I'd like to see them try doin' that to me," Hunter siad boastfully.

"Oh, yea, like you could hold off a bunch of seniors on your own," Trent rolled his eyes.

"You might be surprised," Hunter siad.

"I think you might be surprised," Trent said.

"Sometimes I'd like to shove you in a toilet," Hunter said under his breath.

Hunter unlocked his phone, but quickly realized there was no reception. "In the middle of the city?" he asked himself, "I thought we were back from the wilderness."

He spoke out loud now, "Well, looks like we're both gonna have a bad day," Hunter told Trent, "Cell service is out."

"What?" Trent questioned, taking out his own phone.

"Shouldn't you be watching the road?" Hunter asked.

"I can watch both," Trent insisted, looking back and forth from the road to his phone. They came to a stop at a redlight.

"Ugh!" Trent grunted, tossing his phone into the cupholder between them.

"It's not the end of the world," Hunter said.

"It might as well be," Trent replied, "I was expecting a call."

"From your *girlfriend*," Hunter teased.

"Doesn't matter," Trent grunted.

Hunter opened his mouth to tease him some more, but he was met with his brother's "stop it" glare. Hunter raised his hands in surrender and leaned back in his seat.

In the silence, he noticed that uneasy feeling again, deep in the pit of his stomach. It was as if he had lived this day before and knew something terrible was just around the corner. However, it was like trying to remember the details of a dream. He could feel the emotions so real, but the images just weren't there.

He told himself that what he had seen on the news was just another blurry video. It didn't mean anything. The U-shape was a simple one to animate - easily faked and easy to imagine. It didn't have any connection to the real U-shaped aircraft he had seen and certainly had nothing to do with The Organization or Daniel.

As he was reassuring himself, they arrived at Boulder High School. They drove into the parking lot and found a space close to the student door.

The brothers got out of the vehicle. Hunter opened the back door and got out his backpack, and Trent did the same on the opposite side. As the two made their way toward the door, Hunter spied Brady and Austin coming from the other direction.

"Later!" Hunter told his brother, and ran off to meet his friends.

"Don't be late this afternoon or you'll be walking home!" Trent warned.

Hunter ignored him.

"Mornin' fellas," Hunter greeted.

"Hey, Hogan!" Austin replied as Brady greeted him with a high five.

"Ready to take on a new adventure?" Hunter asked eagerly.

"I've hardly recovered from the last one," Brady said tiredly.

"Oh, come on," Hunter urged, "It's gonna be great!"

"That's a mighty big mood swing from someone who was fretting over this last week," Brady pointed out.

"I guess I'm just gaining confidence," Hunter said.

"Well, don't get too excited yet," Austin warned, "We still don't have our schedules."

The three reached the entrance and walked through the double doors. They opened to a long hallway that ran alongside the gym. Past that was the lunchroom where most of the students were congregating. The rumble of the surrounding conversations filled the hall.

Hunter had only been here once before when he and the rest of the Freshman class came for orientation. The school wasn't huge, but it was large enough to get turned around in. This part was simple though: find a seat in the lunchroom and wait for someone to say what to do next.

So far, the scenery was everything the movies would have you believe about highschool. The football jocks congregated in one corner of the room being rowdy and goofing off. A herd of preppy blondes giggled and snarked at a similarly obnoxious group of brunettes. The 'band kids' took a whole table to themselves and showed each other their instruments and playing cards.

It took a bit of searching, but the three friends finally found a suitable place to sit, far enough away from people to not look like they were encroaching on another group, but close enough that they didn't look like outcasts.

The three sat and chatted about what they thought the day would hold. They shared rumors they had heard about the best and worst teachers to have. They also speculated which groups of people they would want to be near and who to stay away from.

These conversations didn't last long before the bell rang and a voice played over the intercom, "All first year students, please report to the home-side bleachers in the gym. All other students follow your schedules to your first block class."

The already lively room sprang into action as people moved about, making for their destinations. The three friends followed the crowd to the gym. Hunter recognized some of the people here. Some were from his middle school. Others he had played against at different times during his baseball career. And some had been in his tour group for orientation. Most however, he had never seen before.

The students filled in the bleachers. Hunter and his friends took seats on the fifth row from the floor.

"You think we'll get any classes together?" Brady asked.

"We all have to take Wellness and those are big classes," Hunter said, "There's a pretty good chance we'll get that together."

"Well, there's always baseball," Austin said, "We'll at least be doing that together."

Austin's comment damaged Hunter's optimism. At the moment, Hunter didn't see any way he could hide his powers and play baseball. Over the past few days he had considered revealing the secret in order to play, and deduced that if he did, he would likely not be allowed to because of the advantage that the powers gave him. Either way, he wouldn't get to be on the team. He knew he would have to tell his coach, his parents, and worst of all, his friends, but how he would do that and what excuse he would make were difficult to think about.

The thought saddened Hunter, and he didn't want to think about it. He wanted to focus on making the best of High School. Hunter quickly changed the topic.

"I heard the wellness coach is super tough," Hunter commented, "That's what Trent says anyway."

"Like, lots of push ups and stuff?" Brady questioned.

"Yea," Hunter agreed, "He said he makes you work out the whole block."

Their conversation continued and hopped from subject to subject. They didn't notice it for a while, but there was a group of administrators near the door of the gym. As Hunter sat, he noticed their stances and facial expression becoming more and more nervous. The adults shifted on their feet and rubbed their hands together nervously. Their eyebrows scrunched and beads of sweat formed on their forehead.

Slowly the room of freshmen began to grow ancy as they awaited direction for where to go or what to do next. An hour ticked by and still no word from anyone.

"What do you think's going on?" Brady questioned his friends.

"Maybe somebody's in trouble," Austin suggested.

"That kind of trouble would have us in a lock down," Hunter pointed out.

"There's probably a bunch of cops right outside the gym doors," Austin countered, "They're just keeping us in here so they know where everyone is."

"Maybe there was a problem printing our schedules," Hunter suggested.

As they speculated, finally, A bald man walked out onto the gym floor holding a microphone. Hunter recognized him as the principal.

The man tapped the microphone to make sure it was on. The thud echoed through the gym and a hush fell over the crowd of eagre freshmen.

"Good morning everyone," the principal said, "On behalf of all the staff here at Bounder High school I would like to welcome you to your first day. For those of you that don't know or don't remember, I am Mr. Owens, the principal here. Now, I do have a bit of bad news. I intended to come out here and give you instructions on how to receive your schedules, but there seems to be an area wide internet blackout. It seems to be affecting... everything. Nothing is working."

The friends exchanged glances as a wave of chatter spread through the crowd. Brady and Austin's were looks of disappointment, but Hunter's was one of worry. He couldn't even be happy that he guessed the problem right. His optimism was quickly fading. Too many strange things were happening today for him to ignore. He needed to talk to ALI.

"Now, everyone, everyone listen," Mr Owens waved his hands trying to get the crowd to settle down, "This is what's going to happen. I need you to pay attention," the crowd hushed, "In a few moments, an announcement is going to be made dismissing all those who can drive. I know that all of you are too young to drive, so if you have a sibling you can ride with, you will be dismissed at that time. Now, the phones are also down. So if you do not have a sibling to ride with, I'm sorry, but, you are just going to have to wait here until your parents come to get you at the end of the day."

The crowd was unsettled now. For people like Hunter this was good news, but people like his friends (the majority of the crowd) were going to have to wait here.

"Oh come on!" Austin complained. He looked at Hunter, "You lucky dog."

"Maybe You guys can ride back with me and Trent," Hunter suggested, "They'll never know."

"That's true," Brady said, "We can walk home from your house."

The principal spoke over the crowd, "Please wait here, and we will give announcements over the intercom with updates."

It wasn't long before the announcement came dismissing everyone. Brady and Ausin exited with the crowd and made for the parking lot. It was an act that, to them, felt like quite the rebellious move, but in reality gained no attention.

They reached the jeep and waited for Trent.

"Well, I have to say, I think the first day of highschool was a success," Brady joked.

Hunter wanted to smile, but that uneasy feeling he had been fighting all morning had returned and this time, it wouldn't leave. Something was off. No matter how much optimism he threw at it or how many times he lied to himself that it wasn't there, something was off.

Then another sense kicked in. He sensed something coming toward them from the other side of the school. Seconds after he felt it, he heard it. A low rumble that grew to a roar as it approached. It captured the attention of everyone in the parking lot and all eyes turned to the sky.

Coming over the school was a huge fleet of helicopters. Some were black hawks, others ospreys. They were low enough to see the lettering on the sides: "UNITED STATES MILITARY". The power of their engines shook the ground as they passed by. Awe and confusion filled most onlookers, but Hunter was filled with terror. Was this the infamous Organization? Had they come for him? Were they taking over?

Hunter pressed himself against the Jeep as if it could somehow hide him. His terror turned simply to unease as the helicopters passed over and their roar grew dimmer.

"Wow," Austin siad. It wasn't often that the military flew over this area. It was a sight most there had never seen.

"Where do you think they're headed," Brady questioned.

"I'd say Denver," Trent said, walking up to the Jeep, "That's the only thing in that direction, and it explains why they were so low. They're going in for a landing somewhere."

"I wonder if it has something to do with the internet thing," Brady suggested.

93

"Can we just go home," Hunter said, not wanting to spend another second out here before talking to ALI. Maybe he could ease Hunter's mind or at least confirm that his fears were justified.

"Scared, hotshot?" Trent said.

"I'm cautious," Hunter corrected, wanting to sound braver than he was, "Communications are down and the military's flying around. It seems a little suspicious, doesn't it?"

"Well, if you put it that way," Trent conceded, "Hop in losers. Y'all can hang out at our house until your parents get home."

Everyone climbed into the Jeep and Trent pulled off, fighting the traffic out of the parking lot.

Everything seemed to be normal on the way home. No more aircraft flew over. The streets were calm. Even the weather was nice. White puffy cows dotted the blue sky, occasionally blocking the sun. It just seemed like any other day.

It wasn't enough to ease Hunter's worries. The conspiracy filled conversations on the way home didn't help either. Austin speculated that we were already under attack.

Brady suggested that the government could still get out an emergency broadcast even if communications were down, and that the internet blackout was just a faulty software update. Countering that the helicopters flying over was just a pre scheduled training maneuver.

Trent, just wanting to stir the pot, claimed that aliens had invaded and knocked out our communications, and speculated that they were already attacking Denver.

To Hunter, any theory was as good as the next. There really was no information to base any claim off of. ALI was the only one who might know something. That's why he had to talk to ALI. Maybe he had gained some information through his own means.

The crew pulled into the Hogan's driveway and exited the Jeep. Hunter made sure to grab his backpack out of the back and left everyone else behind.

He barged in the front door and went straight to his bedroom. Though there was no internet, he had downloaded a playlist a while back which worked offline. He connected it to a bluetooth speaker next to his bed and turned the volume up as loud as he could.

He then retrieved the puck from his backpack and went to his bathroom, locking the door to both his room and Trent's from inside. He sat the puck on the vanity.

"ALI," he whispered, "I need your help. Do you know what's going on?"

ALI voice came from puck, "It would seem the entire internet system as well as the entirety of radio and satellite communications went dark a few minutes after you left home this morning."

"Any idea what caused it?"

"I wish I didn't, but I believe I do," ALI answered.

"Well, come on," Hunter urged, "We don't have much time. My friends are over."

"I was able to break into the military's system. It seems they have gone mostly dark as well, but their most recent transmissions were reports of massive ships flying over Montana. Their descriptions matched those of Organization cruisers."

"What are those?"

"Those are massive flying battleships, capable of defeating entire armies and destroying entire cities. They are equipped with technology far more advanced than anything you have ever seen. The only way to defeat a cruiser is with a cruiser and unfortunately that is not a technology that the United States possesses."

"So it was all true," Hunter breathed. He leaned over the vanity, rocking back and forth. He feared for himself, but also what would happen to those around him. The stories ALI had told him of what The Organization could do were nothing short of horror stories. They had

95

seemed so distant then. Hunter never thought he would be feeling the effects of them.

"I'm shocked you doubted me," ALI said.

"Well, sorry if it all seemed a little bit outlandish," Hunter was now packing back and forth across the white tile floor, "Can you contact Daniel?"

"I've already tried. The Organization didn't just bring down communications. They're jamming them."

"But we're safe here. Right?"

"I have no way of answering that."

Hunter stared into the mirror, looking deep into his own blue eyes. Beads of sweat appeared on his forehead. He couldn't help but wonder if he should have gone with Daniel when he had the chance.

He caught himself beginning to spiral. His thoughts were becoming unfocused as fear clouded his mind. He had to stop himself. He closed his eyes and took a few deep breaths. He ran through the facts.

Something big and dangerous was flying over Montana. He trusted ALI's report. It wasn't clear, but it seemed as though The Organization was executing its planned takeover. However, the world is a really big place, so he wasn't necessarily in imminent danger. He had to look through eyes that weren't his own. As far as the world was aware, he was just a normal 13 year old. If he didn't have powers, he wouldn't think he was in danger, so he shouldn't consider himself in danger now. The best thing to do was wait.

Hunter placed the puck in his back pocket and left the bathroom with anxious anticipation for what would happen next. When he opened the door, he saw Brady sitting on his bed holding the speaker. When he saw Hunter he turned it off, stopping the music.

"Everything okay, Hunter," Brady asked.

Hunter hated how he could do that. It was a side effect of growing up with someone, especially someone like Brady. He always knew if something was bugging Hunter.

"Yea, of course," Hunter lied, "What makes you say that?"

Hunter instantly regretted asking the question.

"Well," Brady replied, "It just seems like, for the past week, you swing from being super excited to being super anxious, and honestly I'm getting whiplash. On top of that you seem paranoid. I also noticed that you were sneaking off during the camping trip at night, kind of the same way you snuck off just now, only you were much easier to follow. So, you wanna tell me what's wrong?"

Hunter stared blankly at Brady. A few days ago, he would have given up and told him the secret. He had basically figured it out anyway. But now the secret was more important than ever. Their safety depended on the secret.

"Yes, but I can't," Hunter sighed. There was no gaslighting Brady. The only option was to admit that something was wrong, just that he couldn't say what.

Brady stood up, "Hunter, whatever it is, it's safe with me. We can work through it."

Hunter looked away from Brady and out his bedroom window, not at anything specific, he just didn't want to look at Brady. He feared that even looking in his eyes would give away the secret.

Hunter sensed Brady walking toward the door then turned back, "Well, if you change your mind, you know where to find me."

Hunter was truly thankful for a friend like Brady. As he stood, staring at the passing traffic, the overwhelming thought in his mind was "could telling him really hurt?"

Of all the people he could tell, he was most confident that the secret would be safe with Brady. He knew that Brady wouldn't abuse the knowledge in any way. Really, he trusted that nothing would change at all if he told Brady. In fact, sharing it with Brady would make it a lot easier to keep. It wasn't letting the secret out, it would just be getting it off his chest.

After a few minutes of thought, Hunter was convinced that this was the right decision. He couldn't do anything while he was waiting for The Organization's next move anyway. This would help him from getting lost in his anxiety.

Hunter left his bedroom and walked to the living room where everyone else was. Brady and Hunter sat on one end of the couch and Trent sat on the other. Austin was flipping through endless channels of static on the T.V. Trent was trying to get his phone to work. The only one who noticed him enter the room was Brady. Soon all of their attentions turned to something else.

The power went out. The T.V. turned off as did Trents phone, and all of the lights.

"What's this?" Trent said, flustered.

"Must be a problem at the routing station," Austin said.

Hunter bit his lip, knowing exactly what was happening now.

"Hey," Trent said, "You see a ghost or something?"

At first Hunter didn't realize that Trent was talking to him.

"Earth to Hunter," Trent said, waving his arms.

"Huh?" Hunter said when the words registered, "Oh, Uh, no everything's fine. It's just the power. I'm sure it'll be back on soon."

"Trent, why don't you go try swapping out the quantum batteries for ones tied to a different station," Brady suggested, "Surely two aren't down at the same time."

"Guess I gotta do everything around here," Trent complained, standing up, headed for the breaker box in the utility room.

Hunter knew before he went that it wouldn't work. His theory was confirmed when Trent returned.

"Strange," Trent said, "Both stations are dead. I don't ever remember even one going out, do y'all?"

"Maybe it has to do with the internet thing?" Austin said, clearly worried now.

In fact, everyone was clearly worried. Since everything had swapped to quantum batteries, there had never been a power outage. Hunter couldn't even remember the last one. Everyone knew that one station going down could be a fluke, but two hinted at a very large problem. The events of the day were beginning to add up even for those that didn't have any knowledge of The Organization.

It wasn't long after the outage that Hunter's parents returned home. In the hour or so between, the teens had had nothing better to do than speculate. Hunter only listened in silence to the mostly incorrect theories of the other three. Brady spent much of that time looking at Hunter, giving him worried glances.

Upon their arrival, the couple put an end to the conspiracy and assured everyone that this was all just a fluke, though their own nervousness didn't really sell their case. Jack suggested that Brady and Austin go home so that their parents could find them. No doubt they would be returning home soon.

Jack offered to drive and the boys gathered their things. Jack and Austin walked out the door, but Hunter grabbed Brady's arm and pulled him back inside.

"Tell your parents you want to spend the night here," Hunter instructed, whispering in Brady's ear, "Tonight, I'll tell you what's really going on."

Chapter 10

The afternoon crawled by. With the power out, there was very little to do to pass the time so the family resorted to pulling out their box of old board games. While they played, Hunter inquired of what was happening in town.

James said that traffic had been horrible and the roads were a mess. Over the past few years, many cars had switched to running on quantum batteries, so when the power went out, the cars died. This had caused lots of wrecks and blocked roadways.

Gracie said that she had spoken with an officer who told her the police were having a hard time keeping up because their radios went down with everything else. They had to rely on trucker's Ham radios or just happening upon wrecks to even know that they happened.

Thankfully the Hogans still had cars that ran on gas. Jack suggested that, if everything wasn't back to normal, he would go into town in the morning to fill up some gas cans and grab some food.

At about 7:00 pm there was a knock at the door. Jack answered it and revealed Brady standing a bit anxiously on the other side. Hunter sprang from his chair at the dining room table.

"Hey, Brady," Jack greeted, "What are you doing here?"

"My mom said I could come over here to hang out since y'all are just a few houses down," Brady answered. Jack invited him in and moved out of the doorway. Hunter had made his way across the room to the back door of the house.

"Let's go play catch," Hunter said, opening the door and stepping into the back yard. He left the door open behind him and Brady followed.

The backyard was long and narrow, and had a tall, white privacy fence that enclosed it. Toward the back there were two large oak trees. The rest of the yard was open.

Beside the door was a plastic crate that held a few baseballs and gloves. The boys each took a glove and Hunter took out a tarnished, dirty ball. As they each stooped over the crate, Hunter whispered, "Walk to the back of the yard. We'll toss and talk."

Brady did as he was instructed without a word. Hunter noticed the worried look on his face. Hunter found himself wondering what was going on in Brady's mind. Was he just confused? Was he fearful for the wellbeing of his friend? As they reached the back, they turned to face each other and locked eyes.

As they did, Hunter felt an emotion that was not his own. Though, he didn't feel it, more accurately, he sensed it. It was like fear, but not crippling. Concern.

Hunter squinted his eyes at Brady. The sense grew stronger. He began to feel anxiousness and suspicion. Then, frustration overshadowed the rest.

"Well?" Brady said calmly.

Hunter was shaken from his concentration and the sensation subsided. "Oh, right," Hunter said, sending the discovery of his new ability to the back of his mind, "Well, where do I start?"

Brady watched on, waiting patiently for Hunter to open up, then offered a suggestion, "The beginning is always a good place."

"Right," Hunter acknowledged, "Well, you remember the crystal, and the temple, and the explosion?"

"Of course,"

"Well…" Hunter tossed the ball to Brady, then stretched out his right hand and levitated the crystal from his back pocket, summoning it to his hand. He allowed it to hang in the air, blocked from the view of the window by his body. The green energy began to spread over his arm, but before it could become too visible, he clenched his fist around the crystal and stopped calling for its energy.

Brady's eyes were wide and his mouth hung open. The ball he had caught fell from his hand, "This is what's been making you act so weird?" he inquired.

"Partially," Hunter said, "But the other part is what happened after everything you know about."

Hunter proceeded to explain the events of the night he had received his powers. He spoke of Daniel's visit and the gifts he had left behind. He told why he was keeping the secret, and why he had been sneaking off. Then, he began to tell him everything ALI had said about The Organization.

How Daniel had fought them in secret for years. How they were almost ready to take over the world. How they sought out crystals and crystal bearers to experiment on. How they had technology beyond anyone's wildest imaginations.

"And I really didn't even think I believed it all until today," Hunter explained, "Now, I know it's true."

"But how do we know this Daniel person isn't really the bad guy, trying to keep you from getting involved?" Brady pointed out.

"I've asked myself the same question over and over," Hunter admitted, "I keep coming back to the fact that he could have killed me or taken me hostage, and he didn't. He could have killed you and Austin, but he didn't. Plus, everything he said seems to have come true."

Brady backed up to lean against the fence, "So the world is being taken over..." he commented in disbelief, "And you have superpowers..."

Hunter walked to lean next to him, "Not exactly how I expected High School to go."

"Yea..." The two stared blankly ahead of them, then Brady turned to Hunter, "Nothing's ever going to be the same again, is it?"

Hunter turned to lock eyes with him. They each shared a pain in their eyes, a fear for what was to come. "No," Hunter bit his lip, "Not any time soon."

102

The boys spent the rest of the daylight tossing the ball and talking. It didn't take them long to distract themselves with happier questions, such as Brady asking what powers Hunter had.

It grew dark by about 9:00 and the boys decided to head inside. The house appeared empty when they entered. The rest of the family had seemingly decided to turn in early out of boredom. Hunter walked through the dark room, over to the couch and sat down facing the blank T.V.

Brady followed, stumbling over the coffee table. As Brady fell, Hunter used his powers to redirect him onto the couch cushion beside him. The green aura lit up the room momentarily, then abruptly faded. He didn't want to risk exposing his secret to the rest of the family.

"Woah," Brady breathed, "That was awesome."

"You think that was awesome, you should see what I can really do," Hunter boasted, "*That's* awesome."

"Well, go on," Brady urged, "Show me something else."

"I don't know…"

"Come on," Brady said, "Everyone's in their rooms. Something small won't hurt."

"Fine," Hunter said, actually excited to finally be able to show off. He looked around and spied his mom's house lily growing in the window seal of the dining room. The poor thing had been mostly neglected, wilting and dying in its pot.

Hunter rolled over the back of the couch and walked to the kitchen sink where he made a glass of water. Then, he took it over to the window seal and poured it over the plant. Brady watched over the couch in anticipation.

Hunter looked down the hall to make sure no one was watching, then summoned the crystal's power. Its glowing patterns flowed over his chest and his right arm, which he stretched over the poor plant.

Instantly, it began to perk up. Its leaves returned to their natural posture and began to grow, filling in the empty space of the pot. From the center of the plant sprouted a bud that stretched up above the leaves and opened, revealing a white lily. Once this was done, Hunter allowed the energy to fade.

Brady looked on in amazement, his eyes wide as saucers. Hunter couldn't help but beam with happiness. Maybe the world was ending, but the weight of his secret didn't feel so heavy anymore. He hadn't even realized how separated and alone he had felt since receiving his powers. He only noticed it now that it was gone. His heart was full.

"Wow," Brady exclaimed.

"Yea, that's what I thought the first time I did it," Hunter said, "Only problem is, if I make it too big, it runs out of nutrients and dies."

"Like the tree in the cave you told me about," Brady said, connecting the dots.

"Exactly," Hunter said.

"So, give me something else," Brady requested, "What about the... shield. You were telling me you just figured out how to do that."

Hunter breathed through his teeth. It was definitely something safe to demonstrate in the house, but it was probably the most difficult thing he knew how to do. "I can try."

Hunter held out both of his hands in front of him, allowing the energy to return. It flowed down both arms now, creating green lines and angles as it went.

"Imagine it condensing and spreading out from your fingertips," Hunter told himself, repeating ALI's coaching. He closed his eyes and began thinking of what he wanted his powers to do.

He imagined the abstract shapes and angles moving forward and seeping off his fingertips into the air around him. He imagined the light thickening and condensing into a tangible sheet. He imagined the sheet growing, until it was a wall in front of him.

104

When he opened his eyes, that was exactly what he saw. A rectangular wall of energy had appeared, just big enough to separate Hunter and Brady. In the center, the energy was a deep solid green, translucent in nature. Near the fringes the energy grew brighter, thinner, and lighter with frills and waves of energy pulsing through it.

Brady, not understanding what would happen, gently tossed the baseball from earlier at the shield. Before Hunter realized what he had done, the ball made contact with the shield and deflected off with great force.

Brady ducked as the ball flew over his head. Seeing the ball was headed straight for the big screen television a few feet away, Hunter dissolved the shield and thrust his hand toward the ball. Before the energy of the shield had completely left the air, Hunter had locked onto the baseball meir inches away from the screen.

A green glow surrounded the ball and guilt surrounded Brady. "Oops," he wheezed, "Hunter, I'm sorry, I didn't..."

Brady's heartfelt apology was cut off by Hunter's laughter. Brady only looked at him with a puzzled expression. Hunter pulled the ball through the air and to his open hand, holding it up as if it were a trophy, "Brady," Hunter said smiling, "It's fine. Supersences, remember? That's the first time I've actually saved something!"

Brady cracked a smile, "Well, All hail the world's first real superhero!"

Hunter took a bow, "And I promise to protect this city," Hunter placed the baseball over his heart, "with my life."

Brady placed the back of his hand on his forehead and flopped over on the couch, "Oh, I'm swooning!" he teased.

The two began to laugh at themselves and continued making jokes. Hunter taking on the role of the saving superhero and Brady the impressed innocent bystander.

When their childish game of makebelieve wound down, they found themselves sitting next to each other on the couch. As the laughter died down, a more serious tone came from Brady.

"If all of this is true, are you actually planning to protect Broulder...with your life."

Hunter thought for a moment. He had considered the question before, but the answer felt more obscure now. Then, out of seemingly nowhere, the answer came to him, so clear he knew beyond a doubt that it was true, "Not Boulder," he answered, "But my family, yes."

"Do you think it will come to that?" Brady asked.

"I hope the fighting happens far from here," Hunter said, "What would they want with Boulder anyway? So long as they don't know I exist. I think we are just waiting to see how everything plays out."

"I hope that Daniel guy wins," Brady said.

"For our sake, I do too," Hunter agreed, "Maybe I wouldn't have to hide if he won," He paused, "But ALI makes it sound like he's going to have to lose before he wins."

"What makes you say that?" Brady asked.

"I don't really know. Something about Daniel's resistance breaking up, and Daniel having some long-haul plan to reunite them and the military... or something like that. I don't know. ALI claims he doesn't know very much because he's just a copy of the real ALI."

"I wish you could contact him," Brady said.

"Yeah, me too." Hunter sighed, "I waited too long and now it's too late. We're on our own."

"Well, we've got each other." Brady said, repeating the cliche.

"Well, that's something," Hunter said, "But I'm pretty sure that can't protect us from The Organization."

After this, the boys sat in silence for a bit, thinking about what the future could hold. Then, Brady, forgetting Hunter didn't really need much sleep, suggested they get some sleep. Hunter agreed, though he knew he would be up for a while.

Brady went to the guest room across the hall from Hunter's and there they told each other goodnight and went into their rooms.

Hunter decided to take a shower. The water wasn't hot because of the power outage, but it had managed to hold onto some heat, so it wasn't a miserable experience. After this he took out the puck and continued his lessons with ALI.

He almost went to get Brady, but decided not to. It was late and it had been a long day. He thought it was better that Brady sleep for now.

Tonight's lesson from ALi was different from the ones of hidden world history he had received, such as the true reasons for the Crusades or how Hitler had been in possession of some of the crystals at one time. Tonight ALI gave Hunter a warning.

"Hunter, I need you to listen closely,"

"Yea, ALI, what's up?"

"Everything is up," ALI said, concern dotted his automated voice, "There was transmission sent out to the world earlier today. You need to listen."

Audio began to play from the puck, above which ALI's round emblem floated. There was a bit of static, but through that, he could hear the emotion filled voice of a young man who spoke with a slight southern drawl, "My father was the smartest man I've ever known. Everything he did, he did with purpose.

I stand before you, not wanting the title of leader, yet still seeking it, because like you, I trust my father. And I want the same thing he did," there was a pause and the inflection of his voice changed, "to see The Organization burn. They have lurked in the shadows for centuries and destroyed the lives of nearly every citizen of the world in one day. They have sought to take everything that I hold dear, and seek to take it from you as well.

My father was a fighter, and a unifier. I hear stories of how he once united the world together against the Organization when they were in the shadows, yet now we can't seem to agree to unite against them?

Disunity has no place in this effort. And if you can't unite behind me because you don't know me, then I understand, but you should at least be able to unite behind me because you knew my father."

There was another pause and when the voice came back it was lass angry and more authoritative, "So with that I make a plea to all those who knew my father, and every nation plagued by these attacks, and all those who want to see every Organization ship fall out of the sky, and to all those who want to be free, come to this base and join us. Together, we will make them pay for what they have stolen, and we will take it all back as one Ekklesia. We will make their world rule the shortest in history.

And to The Organization who is no doubt seeing this and trying to turn it off, I invite you here as well in the entirety of your might. Come see what happens when you tick me off. And better yet, see what happens when you tick US off."

There was a final pause. This was a long one. When the voice came back, it was a bit shaky and quieter, in a way that promised retribution, "And to the one who killed my father, The Parasite, stop your cowardly mind games and come face me."

The transmission ended and Hunter sat back on his bed. It was quite a lot of information to process and for the most part it didn't make sense. "What was that?" Hunter asked.

"That was the voice of Daniel's son, Dylan," ALI explained, "It seems as though Daniel has been killed by another crystal bearer we call The Parasite."

Hunter's eyes grew wide. If The Organization was powerful enough to kill this man, how could he hope to fight or even hide from them?

ALI continued, "He left the coordinates of Daniel's secret base. I see only two options. Either we flee to the mountains where you found the crystal or we join Dylan and help him fight. The rhetoric of the message seems to imply a boulder takeover than I anticipated. I feel that we are no longer safe here if The Organization defeats Dylan."

Hunter didn't really know what to say or think. It didn't seem Dylan stood much of a chance to him, but if he could help, he might be able to make a difference in the outcome of a battle. On the other hand, it would probably be much safer for his family to hide in the mountains. There was a chance they could live in the cave he had discovered and go undetected. He knew he couldn't make this decision on his own.

"ALI, I think it's time to let my family in on the secret."

Chapter 11

Hunter spent the rest of the night going over his options with ALI. Hunter had truly grown to trust his AI companion and felt that his insights offered an outside perspective while still being concerned for the well being of all involved. He was analytical, but surprisingly human-like.

Hunter had to consider all of his options, the first being whether or not to tell his family, which he had mostly already decided. Hunter knew his mom would never support him going to fight even if it did turn out to be the right decision. Really, he didn't think her overly emotional character would be much help at all. Still, he wouldn't think of doing something without her knowing.

What made the decision clear was that, more than anything, he needed his dad. His dad would be level headed and, more than anyone, he would know what to do and how to react.

Hunter also had to consider which option, hide or fight, he most supported. ALI clearly wanted to fight. He wanted to finish what his maker started and believed that Hunter's crystal could be instrumental in doing just that. Hunter didn't know what to think. He knew the only way he would go was if the ones he loved went to hide in the hidden world of the cave. He couldn't take them into a war zone, and he couldn't leave them where they would be in possible danger. Plus, he had no idea how to fight. He barely knew how to use his powers. What help could he be?

He toiled on this wise all night. Stay or go? Stay or go? Ultimately, he knew the decision would come down to what his dad had to say. Knowing everyone needed the rest, including himself, Hunter gave into sleep just as the first notes of sunlight began to peek through his blinds.

***

Hunter's eyes fluttered open. The time had come. His plan was to first go to his dad and then have him let the rest of the family in on what was happening.

Hunter rolled out of bed, anxiety squeezing his chest. He got dressed. No sounds came from the rest of the house. Not that anything was working to make noise.

Once he was dressed, he took the crystal from his night stand, closed it in his fist, and walked out of his room, across the house. He headed for the master bedroom which was on the opposite side of the home from his room, on the other side of the kitchen.

Sunlight poured through the blinds now. It had to be at least 9:00 am. He sensed someone ahead of him as he came down the hallway and found his mom sitting on the couch reading a book.

"Goodmorning hun," she greeted.

"Morning, Mom," Hunter replied, "Hey, do you know where dad is?"

"I believe he's out back," she said.

"Thanks."

Hunter turned from his planned route and headed for the back door. He opened it and found his dad sitting in a lawn chair, sipping luke-warm apple juice from a mug. He turned to see his son.

"Good Morning, Hunter," Jack said.

"Hey, Dad," Hunter replied. He stood there awkwardly for a moment, looking for the words he had rehearsed all night, "So... I need to tell you something."

"Okay, son," Jack answered, keeping his relaxed tone, "Have a seat." He gestured to a closed lawnchair that leaned against the house.

"Actually, I think I'd better stand," Hunter said.

"Ok," Jack said, more interested, but still calm.

Hunter walked in front of his dad's chair and stood there, "So, I think sometimes it's easier to show than explain," Hunter said.

He held out his hand and revealed the glowing green crystal. His dad examined it, clearly failing to see its significance. Then, Hunter allowed the energy to spread across his upper body.

Now, his father's eyes grew large as he nearly became strangled on his juice. He leaned back in his chair in wonder, barely holding onto his usual collected composure.

From there Hunter explained everything, very similar to how he had explained it to Brady the night before, now including the part about the message he had received, and the decision he had to make.

About an hour passed as the two talked and the long morning shadows grew shorter. His dad never once expressed disbelief, but listened intently to Hunter's explanations trying to learn what his son already knew. Finally, Hunter had finished his summary and dad had asked all of his questions. Now, the two stood in silence, Hunter waiting for direction and Jack looking for direction to give.

Finally, he spoke, "Son, I think it would be unwise for you to try and fight. You have no experience and it would be very difficult for you to get to the hidden base anyway. What I think we should do is tell the family and prepare to give that cave of yours a visit. If things go south here, we'll be ready at a moment's notice to leave. Your robot friend can help us get information about what's going on, and then, if we can find a way to contact this Dylan, we can offer him your crystal in exchange for protection."

Hunter liked this answer. Somehow his dad had found a way to check all the boxes. Everyone could stay safe and stay together, plus, they might be able to help in the fight against The Organization.

"Alright," Hunter said, "Let's do it...but you have to tell Mom."

The two smiled. "Ugh, fine," his dad joked, "Let's go inside and we'll make a plan for today, then see what happens from there. Sound good?"

"Sounds good."

Jack stood up and followed Dylan inside the house. He kept a very calm composer, but his face had turned pale. Gracie still sat on the couch reading her book, but looked up when they walked in.

"Well, boys, how was the talk?" she asked.

"Good," Jack replied, "but you should go get Trent... and Brady while you're at it. We're having a family meeting."

"Is everything okay?" Grace asked, quickly standing up and tossing her book aside.

"It should be, but this is important," Jack urged.

Gracie shook her head and speed-walked down the hallway, nearly in a tizzy. "Well, you already scared her," Hunter said, plopping down on the couch.

"Might as well go ahead and get it out of the way," Jack replied, walking to stand in front of the T.V., the place from which he would conduct the meeting.

Hunter was surprised that he felt such anxiety now as opposed to when he was talking to his dad. Of course, he had been nervous, but now he felt the weight of a new responsibility. He had to keep everyone safe. Any target that was on his family would be because of him and him alone. Any move he made, now more than ever, would carry grave consequences, and would have to be done with the utmost care and consideration.

Gracie returned with a confused Brady and a grumpy Trent. Brady and Hunter locked eyes. He must have known exactly what the meeting was about. From his perspective, it probably looked like a complete 180. Just the night before Hunter was still trying to hide this secret from his family. Now, he was about to reveal it to everyone.

Brady sat next to Hunter and Trent next to him. Grace sat on the other section of the couch next to her book. Once everyone was settled in, Jack started the meeting, "Well, everyone, I guess to begin, some things are easier to show than explain," He locked eyes with Hunter, "Son, could you show everyone."

Hunter stood up and pulled the crystal from his pocket.

"Wait!" Trent exclaimed, "What if some of us don't want to see it?"

"Trent," his father barked, "Behave! This is very serious."

Trent cowered, "Yes, sir, sorry." He slumped down on the couch and gave Hunter his attention, as did the rest of the family.

Hunter closed his eyes, and not meaning to, sensed the emotions of those in the room. Trent mostly radiated regret and embarrassment. From Brady came mostly excitement.

From his father came resolve, it stood like a wall concealing what he really felt. Hunter was surprised to find that he could see deeper, past the wall, and found what was actually fear for his family and uncertainty - a drive to lead and protect. A longing to make the right decision when, really, he was filled with confusion.

Seeing this pulled Hunter deeper, as he almost forgot what was going on around him. He could see the gears of his father's mind turning in ways he had never seen them. He couldn't see specific thoughts, but he could feel the emotions that the thoughts brought, all of them, whether fear or hurt or determination, were driven by a love one couldn't sense without looking within.

"Hunter," called the voice of his father.

His eyes opened and met his dad's. "Oh, right," Hunter said. He refocused his mind, opened his hand and revealed his powers once again. He allowed the energy to spread across his entire upper body. He held his arms out to the sides and levitated the radiating crystal in front of his chest.

"Oh! Oh my!" Gracie exclaimed.

"Cool," Trent said in awe.

From there the explanation began once again, Hunter telling most of the story and his dad chipping in here and there to keep him on track. Gracie waited until the end to flood them with questions, but her husband stopped her, promising to fill in as many gaps as he could later as well as promising that Hunter could tell her more when they had time.

"Right now, what we have to focus on is the fact that we don't have any idea what is going to happen next," Jack explained, "We need to prepare to leave if we have to," He turned to Brady, "That includes

114

you. When we're done, you need to go home, and I need to have a talk with your mother."

"Yes, sir," Brady agreed.

"What about Austin?" Hunter asked.

"Only the people that know are in danger, right?" Jack inquired.

"I think so," Hunter guessed. That was the point of not sharing the secret.

"Then we just have to keep it that way," Jack decided, "We can't take extra people with us."

"But Dad…" Hunter started, not wanting to leave his friend behind.

"No," Jack butted in, "We can talk about this later."

Hunter did as he was told, but fully intended to talk about it later. The world was in danger. That included Austin, and Hunter wasn't just going to leave him behind.

"Now," Jack continued, "We have plenty of camping equipment, but we need more non perishables. Trent, I think it would be good for you and Hunter to go into town and get some supplies."

"Jack!" Grace said, "It's dangerous there right now."

"I know honey, but somebody has to and you and I have things to do here. Trent's an excellent driver and he's got a superhero to protect him."

Trent nodded his head and Hunter gave a thumbs up.

"Gracie, I need you to stay here and get everything we might need: tents, sleeping bags, toiletries; all of it needs to be under the carport so we can load it into your van and the jeep when the boys get back."

"Okay," Gracie agreed.

115

"And there needs to be room for people too," Hunter added, only half joking.

"I'll see what I can do," Gracie said, "The superhero might have to ride on the roof." She managed to crack a smile, but it was clearly forced.

"Brady, I'll go with you to try and explain this to your mother," Jack continued, "Which…" he paused and sighed, "is going to be extremely tough without the proof."

He looked at Hunter as he started rethinking his plan.

"I have more proof," Hunter said, perking up, "You can take the puck and ALI. I know you haven't seen that stuff yet, but I promise, it'll be very convincing."

"Okay, then." Jack said, nervously but authoritatively clasping his hands together, "Everyone knows their jobs. Let's get a move on it."

The family stood up from their seats and sprang into action.

"I'm headed for the jeep," Trent said, walking toward the door.

"I'll be there in a second," Hunter replied, "Let me get this for dad."

Trent soluted Hunter, then slipped out the door.

"I'll start a list, then start gathering everything," Gracie said, scrambling into the kitchen.

"Brady, grab a water bottle for me, please," Jack requested, "I'll walk you down to your mom in just a second."

"Yes, sir"

"Dad," Hunter called from his bedroom door.

"Coming, son," he replied.

Hunter swung open the door and summoned the puck to his hand from his nightstand. It flew across the room and reached him just as his dad reached his room.

"ALI," Hunter called, "Show yourself."

The slit on the crystal opened on the puck and the black mist swarmed out from it, forming ALI's circular, slotted emblem in the hallway.

"Yes, sir. How can I help?" ALI said.

Jack must have just been out of emotion to react. His eyes were wide, but his voice and actions were collected, "Yep, nothing surprises me anymore today," he said, putting a hand on his hip, "I think that'll be pretty convincing."

"He can help you explain parts of the story too," Hunter said. He turned his conversation to ALI, "Now, ALI, nothing too detailed and nothing too fancy. Don't scare the lady."

"What lady?" ALI inquired.

"Brady's mom," Hunter informed him, forgetting that he hadn't been at the meeting, "You've got to help Dad convince her of what's actually happening."

"Without you?" ALI asked.

"That's the trick isn't it," Jack said to the AI.

"You've got this," Hunter encouraged them, "ALI, you listen to him. Keep him safe like he's me."

"Of course, sir."

Hunter handed the puck to his dad. ALI's emblem faded and the black dust retreated back inside. Then, the two walked down the hall and to the door where Brady was waiting for them.

"Ready?" Jack asked, not specifically to one boy or the other.

Before they could answer a voice came from the kitchen. "Wait, wait, wait," Gracie called after them, "Come here."

She wrapped the two boys in a hug, perhaps unknowingly, squeezing them as hard as she could. It was a while before she let go, but neither of the boys stopped her. The embrace was warm and comforting. It, if only for a moment, quieted the chaos that was brewing.

When she finally let go, she kissed each boy on the head. Then, she and her husband shared a bit of a longer embrace and a kiss.

"Okay you guys," Hunter said, humorously.

The two let go of one another and smiled. Gracie stood back and looked at the group, tears welled up in her eyes, "Okay, you just be safe," her voice was shaky. She looked at Hunter and gave him another (shorter) hug, "I love you."

"I love you too Mom," Hunter said. He didn't know why, but he got that feeling again. That same feeling from the day before that said something bad was about to happen - that feeling that he had lived that day before. This time, it wasn't ominous. It simply told him to linger in his mother's embrace. So he did.

"Okay!" Grace pushed him away, "Go on, do what you need to do and get back here."

"On it!" Hunter said.

"Yes we are," Jack said enthusiastically, "I'll be back in a few minutes...hours," he threw his hands up, "Who knows? I have to convince my son's best friend's mother that my son's a superhero and the world is ending."

"You've got this, honey" Gracie encouraged as the group walked out the door.

Hunter broke off from his dad and Brady. They were going left to Brady's house, and he was going right to the carport and Jeep.

"Good luck!" Hunter said, waving.

"You too!" Brady replied.

"Make it quick... and don't buy the whole store!" Jack added.

"You got it," Hunter gave a thumbs up.

He turned and met his brother who was already in the driverseat. He walked to the passenger side and climbed in.

Without a word, the two pulled off and started for town. It took a few minutes of driving for Trent to speak. "So you knew all of this, all this time, and chose to just now tell me."

"Well, to be fair, I didn't tell anyone at all until I told Brady last night," Hunter retorted.

"I'm just saying, I'm brother to the first superhero in the world and you told Dad before you told me," Trent said. He was clearly just antagonizing to lighten the mood.

"Well, to be fair," Hunter replied, "I probably would have told you before Dad under normal circumstances."

"Normal as in...?"

"Normal, like, I have powers, but the world's not ending. Still would have told Brady first though."

"That, I can live with," Trent smiled.

The roads leaving the neighborhood were completely clear, but the gravity of what was happening began to set in when they reached town.

Abandoned cars littered the roadway and had been pushed so that only one car could fit down the middle of the road. Many had their windows smashed in where thieves had looted them.

"Come on Boulder," Trent said in disbelief, slowly making his way down the apocalyptic street, "It's only been one day."

119

Before they neared the part of town where the stores were, the slow traffic came to a complete standstill. Horns were honking ahead of them, but after about fifteen minutes, the line hadn't moved an inch.

The architecture here made it difficult to see what was going on ahead. The city was sectioned off into blocks like any other, but the streets were narrow, and the red-bricked buildings were bulky, some feeling like they leaned over the street.

"How far do you think it is to the supermarket?" Hunter asked.

"I don't know, but we're gonna get stuck if we stay here," Trent said, frustrated and nervous.

It just happened that the brothers had come to a stop near an intersection.

"Let's turn off here," Trent said, "We can walk the rest of the way."

Trent backed up a bit to make the turn (thankfully, they hadn't been blocked in yet). The road they turned onto was empty for now, with the exception of a few abandoned cars that sat in the roadway where they died.

Next to the sidewalk, there was a parallel parking spot. Trent pulled in, and the brothers exited the jeep. "I hope there's food left to get," Hunter said.

"We'll be lucky if there is," Trent replied.

The two began to walk toward their destination on the deserted sidewalks. The only sign that humans still lived here was the traffic beside them that still wasn't moving.

Their frustration was clear. Many honked their horns or yelled out their windows at the vehicle in front of them. Many of the storefronts they passed had been boarded up. Not a single one was open and there was no sign of power being on in the whole city.

"Where is everybody?" Trent questioned.

"Staying home because of the outage?" Hunter proposed.

After a few blocks, the brothers walked up on the issue. Across an open square, a herd of people had gathered, shouting and shoving outside of the supermarket. It was just a small, old fashioned general store, but there had to be at least 300 people trying to get in.

"Well, I found all the people," Trent said, astonished.

"Looks like we're gonna have to find a new store," Hunter said.

"Can't you do some kind of Jedi mind trick or something?" Trent asked.

"I have powers from a rock, not the force," Hunter retorted.

"You're not gonna have much better luck anywhere else," a voice said.

It startled the brothers. Both turned to see a middle aged man sitting on a metal bench a few feet ahead of them. He wore a fancy blue suit and tan tie. The tie, however, had been loosened and the top button of his shirt was undone. He sat in a hunched position with both elbows on his knees.

"What makes you say that?" Hunter asked.

"My car went dead yesterday with the rest of 'em," the man explained, "I live too far away to walk home. I've been all over Boulder and watched this happen at all the other places. Started about midnight. Far as I can tell, this is the last one."

"People went crazy that quick?" Trent questioned, "It's just a power outage."

"You haven't heard?" the man asked.

"Heard what?" Hunter asked back.

"Some truckers came into town last night," the man said. His tone took on that of one telling an old ghost story, "Word came over the HAM radio. Massive spaceships flew over the country and duked it out

121

in D.C. Nothin's left. Then, something blew up most of Denver this morning."

Hunter and Trent exchanged worried glances. Fear gripped Hunter and he could feel it radiating off his brother. It was bad enough that Washington was gone, but Denver was too close.

They hardly even have time to think about what they had just heard before a sound caught their attention. The three looked around for the source.

It was a low frequency hum that rose above the bickering crowd before them. It grew louder and closer, but the building beside them was blocking the view.

They only saw the source when they flew over.

Four massive aircraft, tall and slender, slipped just over the top of the building. They were black and had two gun barrels that protruded off the bottom. The top was elongated for a pilot and branching from either side were wings, not longer than the craft was tall, which had a gun on the end of each. The whole thing together created a 'T' shape. Their engines shook the ground with their power. They moved slowly.

Once they were a ways out over the open square, a higher frequency shrill came from the same direction the other ships had come from. These ships were clearly moving faster and zipped over the roof of the building, quickly passing up the other craft.

These were U-shaped like the one Daniel had come in. For a moment, Dylan hoped that the Dylan person he had learned of had come to help him, but something was different about these ships. He hadn't been able to see what color Daniel's ship was in the darkness, but he knew the engines burned yellow. These burned orange.

The angry mob was now silent, their attention locked on the strange ships.

"Friends of yours?" Trent asked.

As if to answer, a black orb was ejected from the shaft of one of the T-shaped ships. It soared through the air and went out of sight for a moment. Nearly as soon as it dipped out of view, an orange sphere expanded outward, over the tops of the building. Though he could see the destruction caused by the sphere, there was an eri silence. Hunter and the crowd watched on in stunned anticipation.

Almost as quickly as it expanded, it collapsed on itself. A deafening explosion rang through the air and the buildings surrounding the explosion were blown to pieces. Flames rose in the distance and the shockwave shattered every window in sight.

"Nope!" Hunter cried, fearing for his life.

Screams of terror erupted from the mob that quickly turned into a stampede. People began running in every direction, seeking shelter from the ominous aircraft.

Hunter and Trent joined in, sprinting for their jeep. More explosions rang out. The T-shaped ships had split up and were raining fire in every direction. Hunter's ears rang as the deafening power of each shockwave nearly knocked him off his feet.

The people stuck in traffic abandoned their still running cars and began running down the streets. One bomb landed a few blocks ahead of Hunter. The orb of energy expanded and contracted, sendings its booming shockwave directly down the street. This caused Hunter to stumble backward. He could hardly gather himself. Fear gripped him. The damage had to be near their vehicle. What if they became stranded in town?

People run around Hunter, slamming into him and tossing him from side to side. One woman ran past and tripped, falling on her face at Hunter's feet. Slowly becoming overwhelmed, Hunter tried to help her up, but she only screamed and crawled away, before making it to her feet.

He hadn't realized, but he had run off and left Trent. Just as he began to grow frantic, frozen and scanning the crowd for his brother, Trent ran up behind him, and placed his hand on his shoulder.

Hunter screamed and pulled away, not realizing who it was. The green energy erupted across every inch of his body. Now the terrified crowd was running away from him, but Hunter didn't notice that part. All he noticed was his brother standing there.

Explosions continued to ring out, but Hunter couldn't hear them anymore. He had completely given into fear. His mind had collapsed in on itself just like the explosions. He could only stand and cry relentlessly.

"Hunter!" His brother cried out. Trent pulled Hunter into an embrace and spoke in his ear, "Alright hotshot, I know you're scared. Me too, but I need you to come back to me. And if those powers are gonna come out to play, now's the time. If not, I at least need you to run."

Hunter took a deep breath. His sanity was returning as his brother grounded him. The explosions once again registered in his mind. Fear gripped him, but now that he had his brother, he wasn't petrified. Trent pushed away from Hunter, but still held his arms.

"You've got this," Trent encouraged, "We're gonna be fine."

Hunter once again examined his surroundings and allowed his powers to kick in. His adrenaline had magnified his senses to a level he had never experienced. He could sense around corners he couldn't see. He could feel where the bombs were going to land before they were shot.

He located each of the four bombers in the sky and determined that they could make it to the jeep. The two ran again, Hunter dramatically slowing his pace to account for Trent. It wasn't that Trent was slow, but rather that Hunter was extremely fast.

Just as they were about a block away, Hunter sensed one of the smaller ships flying up behind them. He skidded to a stop and turned around.

The U-shaped fighter was flying just above the street. It had two guns under its cockpit at the front of the 'U' and was firing on the abandoned cars in the street. The explosions from the orange plasma bolts, combined with the gasoline in the cars caused the explosions to fill up the entire space between the buildings.

The ship was approaching fast and Hunter knew he would only get one shot. He summoned the energy and held both hands out in front of him. He thought of where he wanted the energy to go and aimed as best he could, then released a powerful beam of energy.

It made direct contact with the side of the ship and illuminated a thin orange film on the surface. This film shielded the craft from damage, but the force of the blast shoved into the row of buildings it was flying next to. It exploded through the side and out the top of the concrete building, exiting in two pieces, both of which fell on the next street over.

"Nice shot!" Trent yelled from about ten feet away.

The two met up again and began running. They were now making their way down the only part of the city that wasn't leveled. It appeared that the only ships that had stayed here were the two small ones and on T-shaped ships.

As they ran, the bomber, escorted by the U-shaped ship, appeared ahead of them. Trent looked to Hunter who was purposely staying a few feet behind him. Hunter was still terrified, but was a bit more confident in himself after his success.

The brothers stopped running, and the ships began their attack. The smaller ship sped out in front of the larger, in line with the street.

"Trent, stand behind me," Hunter commanded.

He did as he was told. Hunter then took a few steps toward the incoming vessel. It was as if he and the pilot were in a staring contest. As the U-shaped ship neared, the bomber ejected an orb that quickly passed the jet and was headed straight to Hunter.

There wasn't time to panic. In fact, it was as though instinct took over. In the split second that the orb was in the air, Hunter remembered what he had done with the baseball the night before.

He stretched out his hand and commanded the bomb to bend to his will. Instantly, the bomb froze, bound by the green energy that surrounded it. It hung in mid air about fifty yards from Hunter.

Once he had possession of it, he thrust it at the smaller fighter headed toward them. The pilot tried to pull up, but Hunter caused the orb to follow it. The two met and an orange explosion, riddled with bits of jet, filled the air.

Hunter stood on the ground, his energy radiating from head to toe, the green light shimmering off the broken glass that littered the sidewalk. In the distance, the large ship turned and began to fly in the opposite direction.

Hunter took his eyes off it and looked at Trent. Their eyes locked and a traumatized yet victorious, half-smile spread across both their faces. Just as Hunter was about to make a celebratory comment, he sensed something coming from the sky.

Debris from the U-shaped ship's destruction was raining down. Hunter lifted his hands and did his best to make a shield to cover the two of them. His desperation made the shield spread out quickly, but not quick enough.

A hunk of metal fell from the sky, striking Trent of the head. He fell to the ground as the shield finally covered him.

"Trent!" Hunter called his brother. He was attempting to stand up, but Hunter could see blood coming from his brow.

He wanted to rush over and check on him, but he had to concentrate on the shield. Large chunks were still falling, deflecting off the shield.The rain of shrap metal continued for seconds that felt like hours. One half of the 'U', an engine, fell and crashed through the building next to them, exploding as it hit the ground.

Finally, the shrapnel rain stopped and Hunter rushed to Trent's side. He was now sitting up, holding his head.

"Hey, are you good?" Hunter asked, kneeling down and moving Trents hand out of the way.

This action revealed a gash that stretched from the top of his forehead to his eyebrow, about four inches. It was bleeding profusely, but, judging by the basketball sized hunk of metal next to him, it could have been a lot worse.

"I think I'm fine," Trent said, trying to stand.

"Well, you're bleeding a lot," Hunter said, "Here," Hunter took hold of Trent's shirt and ripped the sleeve off.

"Hey!" Trent complained, woozy, "Destroy your own shirt."

"You're the one that's bleeding," Hunter retorted, pressing the cloth firmly on Trent's wound.

"Oww! Oww!" Trent wined, "Lay off the superstrength!"

"I'm not using superstrength," Hunter said, still pressing the cloth to his complaining brother's head.

"Well, you're still glowing," Trent pointed out, "And that h... Actually, it doesn't really hurt now."

"See," Hunter said, "Don't be a baby."

"No, I mean, I actually doesn't hurt at all," Trent said, perplexed.

He reached up and pulled Hunter's hand and the cloth away.

"Hey!" Hunter said, knowing he needed to hold pressure to stop the bleeding. To his surprise however, all that was there was dried blood and a scab.

Hunter hardly had any emotion left to be surprised. He only stared at the closed wound as Trent examined it with his hand.

"Hunter..." Trent said in disbelief, "You healed me."

"No," Hunter replied thinking hard about the situation, "ALI said I can only speed up what the plant, or I guess, body is doing... I guess I just sped up you healing yourself the normal way."

127

"Either way, everything you just did... was totally awesome," Trent said, cracking the first real smile since the attack.

Hunter smiled back a traumatized smile. Everything that had happened hadn't truly set in. The wound had actually almost made him forget about it.

Now that he was back to reality, and the dust was beginning to settle, and the smoke was beginning to rise, he could think of only one thing. They had to get home – quickly.

Hunter and Tent found their jeep, miraculously shielded from the explosions. The building it had been parked between were some of the only ones still standing.

Everything was coated in a thick grey dust. The once red jeep was now that same dingy grey. The brothers climbed in, and Trent turned on the wipers to clear the windshield.

As they made their way out of town, the magnitude of the devastation began to set in. Entire buildings had been incinerated. Craters dotted the landscape, making the once crammed city look desolate and open, like a barren desert.

Small fires burned here and there. A gentle breeze kicked up ash and dust. The air smelled burnt. Not like a campfire, more like something burning in the oven. It was sharp and pungent.

As the jeep bumped along, people walked along what used to be the sidewalk. Some screamed and wailed over bodies. Others rummaged through the debris. Some sat, huddled under door frames, shaking with fear. All were covered with the grey dust, most were covered with blood.

The sights were gorey and Hunter had to look away, choosing to stare at the floorboard. He could see his brother gritting his teeth, doing his best to focus on driving out of town. Even looking away wasn't enough to shield Hunter, however. The pain of the people rose in a thundering cry only he could hear. He wasn't trying to sense it. He tried to stop, but it was too loud.

Hunter mourned for his city. His stomach twisted and his heart ached. The cries of their fear haunted him. The burning smell sickened him.

As he tried to think of anything else, and failed, a new cry rang out. He sensed great desperation. It was so compelling that it forced him to look up. Through the barren landscape, a little ways ahead on what remained of the sidewalk was a woman. Next to her, a child.

The child was lying on the ground and crying. The woman had lifted his head into her lap and was doing her best to hold pressure on a wound: a gash down the young boy's arm.

"Trent, pull over," Hunter requested.

"I can't," Trent shook his head. HIs voice quivered, "You see the way these people are looking at us? They'll steal the Jeep the second we stop."

"Pull over, Trent!" Hunter said, "I'm going to help that kid."

The jeep was passing them now. Hunter looked at them through the dust-covered window. The woman didn't look up, desperately tending to the child's wound.

"I can't," Trent repeated.

"Then, I'll catch up," Hunter said. He manually unlocked his door and jumped out of the slow moving Jeep.

"Hunter!" Trent yelled, slamming on the breaks.

Hunter hit the ground, stumbling, but able to steady himself. (The Jeep had only been moving about 10 miles per hour). He walked back to the woman. Now, she was the one crying, and the boy was unconscious. She leaned over his body.

"Excuse me," Hunter said, "I think I can help."

The woman didn't acknowledge him and continued to sob, lamenting for her son. Hunter placed his hand on her shoulder and

129

pulled her back a bit, then knelt down next to the boy. He allowed the energy to flow over his right hand.

The boy's wound was on his left forearm, the one closest to Hunter. It was a long, deep gash, going from his wrist, almost to his elbow. He had lost a lot of blood.

Hunter began to question his ability to help the boy, but proceeded quickly. Hunter placed his energy covered hand just above the wound, in the same manner as he would to make a plant grow. He moved it back and forth. The energy spread from his hand to the boy's arm.

When the woman saw what was happening, her eyes grew wide. She didn't understand that Hunter was trying to help her, "My son!" she wailed, "What are you doing to my son!"

She was hysterical, as any mother would be. It startled Hunter, but he did his best to ignore her and focus on what he was doing. She pulled at Hunter's hand, but all her strength was gone.

It didn't take long for the wound to begin to close. The flowing waves of energy seemed to pull the flesh together. The runny blood grew thick and formed a scab. Hunter looked at the boy's face. His eyes were open now. He stirred groggily.

Hunter smiled at his work. He called the energy away and placed his hand on the woman's shoulder. "Ma'am, your son's going to be fine," Hunter consoled.

It must have been a combination of Hunter's words and the boy's slight movements that broke through to the woman. Either way, the realization struck her and her tears of sorrow turned to tears of joy.

"Tyler!" she exclaimed, scooping her son into an embrace. She pulled him away momentarily to inspect his arm. She briefly placed her hand over her mouth in shock, then gave back into embracing her son. "How?" she shook her head and cried some more, "Thank you! Oh, thank you!"

"You're welcome," Hunter said, then walked away.

He was glad he was able to help, but turning back to the damaged landscape brought him back to the reality of what had happened. Hundreds were dead, maybe thousands. More if this had happened in Denver. Everything he knew was gone.

Another reality came to him as well, he had revealed his powers. He had revealed them directly to The Organization. They had left for now, but Hunter had no doubt that they would return.

Hunter ran to the Jeep and jumped into his seat. He expected to hear a reprimand from his brother, but didn't receive one. Hunter looked at Trent and saw he was pail faced and frozen.

"What is it?" Hunter asked.

Trent pointed ahead of them. In the distance, smoke was rising. At first, Hunter didn't know exactly what it was coming from. The devastation and events had him turned around, but he soon realized what it was. It was their neighborhood.

Chapter 12

Trent sped through the rubble as fast as he could and finally exited the devastated town. The road from town to their neighborhood was mostly cleared.

In the distance, the smoke grew closer and the brother's anxiety rose. Fear of what they were driving into was amplified by the devastation they had just experienced. Hunter was mostly scared, but Trent's face showed a level of determination Hunter had never seen in him before. It reminded him of their dad.

The whole way home, Trent prayed under his breath. Trent had always been the religious one of the brothers, and really, of the whole family. Trent and their mom went to church every time the doors were open. Their dad never went to church and Hunter had used that as a way out. Right about now, Hunter was wishing he hadn't.

After what felt like an eternity, they entered the neighborhood. Hunter couldn't help but cry. The houses of his friends and neighbors, the people he had known his whole life had been reduced to nothing but ash and craters. What houses still stood were burning or fallen in.

Trent was forced to stop the jeep because of a massive crater that blocked the road. Frantic, Hunter flung open his door and sprinted through the wreckage. Tears slipped down his cheeks as he tried to find his home.

Why would anyone do this? What could they gain from destroying Boulder, from destroying homes? What world was going to be left for them to take over?

Finally, he reached it. All that was left of his home was the metal carport, now a twisted heap of metal. The home had been stripped to its foundation. Piles of smoldering ash covered what had been the floors. Recognizable fragments of furniture lie tossed about: pieces belonging to the dining room set, a burned couch, half of a bedframe. The crater of the bomb that destroyed his home lay where his neighbors house had been.

Hunter fell to his knees and sobbed. No one could have survived this. The green energy consumed his body uncontrollably. His mind was in agony. Out of the corner of his vision, he saw Trent arrive.

Hunter looked to his brother as the sorrow and anger consumed him as well. He shook his head, "No. No! This isn't..." Tears filled his eyes as he ran off into the rubble of the home. He flipped over pieces of walls and tables searching for peace, but found none. Hunter only cried and watched, knowing there was nothing left to find.

This went on for a while. The pain for both of them was great. It wasn't long though before Trent gave up searching and collapsed in the debris and Hunter had on the street.

He didn't try to compose himself, but for Hunter, the tears eventually stopped. He only stared blankly at what his life used to be – what his life could have, should have, been.

Everyone he and Trent loved were gone. They had nothing left, no way to survive and not much reason to. It was all gone: their parents, their home, their friends. Brady. How could they move on from this? What would be left for them?

His questions and thoughts seemed to dissolve into the same gray shaded ash that covered all of Boulder. The green energy that surrounded him faded into the wreckage that was Hunter's mind.

Just as another wave of emotion and tears began to take over,, he heard a voice. "Hunter? Hunter!" It couldn't be... He turned to look down the street. Running toward him was Brady! Hunter's tired eyes grew wide, and he sprang to his feet.

Faster than he had ever ran before, he sprinted to Brady. They slammed into eachothers open arms and embraced one another. "Brady," Hunter cried, "I thought you were..."

"I thought you were too. When I saw the smoke..."

The two held one another, mourning for what they had lost, but rejoicing they had each other.

"There's nothing," Brady sobbed, "There's nothing left."

They cried until they had no tears left. Snotty, and red eyed, they walked to where the Hogan's house had once stood. Trent walked to meet them.

"Brady," Trent breathed, opening his arms, "It's good to see you." They hugged. Trent, in Hunter's eyes, was unbelievably strong. He was managing to hold his composter while the younger boys still stood on the verge of tears. "How'd you survive?" Trent asked.

Brady gritted his teeth, attempting to build enough courage to tell the story, "I... I was walking back here with Jack when..." he choked back tears, then continued, "We saw the explosions coming from town. Jack told me to hide in the culvert and... and he ran to get Grace."

Hunter was hit with a new wave of emotions, but didn't give into the tears this time. Hunter offered a positive outlook, "Maybe they got somewhere safe too."

Trent's face turned red and he looked away from the group. A tear made its way down his cheek. "What is it Trent?" Hunter demanded.

"I..." Trent tried to catch his breath, "I... Yea... maybe you're right" his voice quivered and his eyes watered.

Hunter came to terms with the reality that he saw Trent knew. If they had made it, they would be here. Hunter began to cry again now. He leaned toward his brother and hugged him. Trent hugged him back and Brady joined in. This would have gone on for a while, but a familiar sound filled the air. It struck terror in all three. Hunter's limbs grew weak as they turned their eyes to the sky.

Descending toward them were three rectangular aircraft escorted by about ten of the U-shaped ships. The boys turned to run, but it was too late for that. The ships were moving fast and surrounded the boys.

The three rectangle ships landed to one side on the cracked pavement and the U-shaped ships swarmed above them. Doors opened on the sides of the rectangle ships and soldiers poured out like ants. They were dressed in all black and wore a metal helmet. They were all holding rifles that resembled the technology Hunter had been given from Daniel.

Hunter didn't know what had come over him, but before he knew it, he was sprinting at the group. Like a wild animal that had been cornered, instinct took over. The crystal's energy surrounded his body once again as he stretched out his hand and released a powerful wave of energy. The wave was wide and moved fast. It struck the soldiers that had exited the nearest ship and thrust them backward, throwing some against the side of the ship.

The rest didn't open fire, but rather, some holding metal rods stepped forward. Hunter stayed back and conjured blasts of energy, shooting them in their direction. Some blasts hit their mark, blowing the recipient backward, but enough missed that some soldiers were able to run up on Hunter.

He could sense their swings and jabs and dodged them. After a moment of this, Hunter saw an opening. He called energy to his fist and lunged at one of the attackers, punching him in the chest and knocking him into a soldier behind him.

While he followed through, one of the other attacking soldiers jabbed the rod at him, hitting him in the side. A powerful blast came from it and flung him through the air. He hit the ground and rolled to a stop near the disfigured carport.

His head was foggy as he looked up, trying to orient himself. He tried to gain his footing, but he was dizzy and fell over. Brady rushed over to help him, to no avail.

"Come on, Hunter!" Brady pleaded, "Get up."

The remaining soldiers with rods were running over to finish the job. Hunter sat up and raised his hand to retaliate. He conjured a blast but it missed by quite a few feet. The whole world was spinning and his vision was doubled.

Just as the soldiers reached them, Trents voice called out.

"Hey!" he yelled.

The exclamation was followed by a gunshot. Hunter rolled over to see Trent running at them with a pump-action shotgun he had seemingly recovered from the rubble.

The soldiers turned their attention to Trent. They walked toward him as he shot. Blast after blast, he rained buckshot on them. They were unphased. Each shot was echoed by multiple sharp "tinks" as their armor absorbed the shot.

Trent began to back up as he shot. "Run!" he screamed.

Hunter's head was still foggy. He knew he had to help, but he could hardly will himself to get up. He rolled over and summoned the energy across his body. As it flowed across him, he felt his strength return. It flowed through his veins and cleared his head. The dizziness left and he pushed himself to his feet.

He looked at his brother who was surrounded. The soldiers stood between them. Hunter sprinted toward the soldiers. As he ran, Trent stopped firing and started running down the road. Hunter reached the soldiers and delivered a powerful punch to each one, throwing them into the destroyed home.

As the three boys ran away, the other soldiers with guns only stood and watched. "What are they doing?" Brady asked, worriedly.

Before Hunter could speculate a red lightning bolt fell from the sky. It struck the pavement between Hunter and Tent and sent the group flying in opposite directions.

Hunter landed on his back next to Brady, quickly rolling over and scrambling to his feet. The green energy still radiated around his body, and he pulled his fists to a fighting position.

Dust had been kicked up from the blast, but through the haze was the glowing red silhouette of a figure. Chaotic arcs of energy jumped from the figure into the air and ground around him. Slowly, the figure raised his hand. Hunter watched in anticipation.

Suddenly, a red blast erupted from the cloud. Hunter formed a square shield, intercepting the blast and quickly countered with a blast of his own. The figure swerved his body to dodge it and stepped out of the dust, revealing another soldier like the rest, only this one wore a glowing red crystal over his chest.

As he stepped forward, he spoke through his helmet which masked his voice, "I've already killed two bearers this week. Surrender, so I don't have to kill another." The man pulled a device from his waistband and from it came a blade, edged with white energy.

As Hunter stood, scared, but prepared to face off against this threat, another shot rang out. The fogg was clearing now and Hunter could see his brother running up on the new soldier shooting the gun. Hunter raised another shield to protect from the overshot.

The red soldier spun around and slashed his sword through the air. He stepped in front of Trent and Hunter lost sight of him. There was a horrible, unnatural "zing", and Hunter saw the front of the gun fall to the ground. It separated into two pieces, separated by a red hot gash. Following this there was a painful wince and a grunt. Hunter gasped as he realized what had happened. Mental agony consumed him as he watched in disbelief.

Trent collapsed onto the ground. The red soldier used his foot to shove Trent's unmoving body into a crater behind him. "No!" Hunter shrieked. His energy engulfed him. The flowing, geometric patterns turned into a raging green inferno. He charged at the soldier, disregarding the threat he posed.

The soldier spun around, but Hunter thrust both fists into his stomach. He was thrown backward, knocking the sword from his hand, and he landed a ways down the road. Hunter advanced, intending to end the fight.

Before he had even taken a step in that direction, something hit Hunter in the back. He felt a part of his body lose its power. Quickly, he spun around and was met with another blast. He stumbled backward. Another one came.

These blasts were black, and he couldn't sense them coming. When they hit his body, his green energy turned black as well and began to flicker and fade.

137

He desperately raised a shield, not finding the source of the attack. He held it, but the first blast that hit it corrupted it, turning it back, then causing it to fade away. He was his again and again. His rage turned to panic. Now more of his body was covered in the black, pulsating void than his own energy.

He slowly lost his strength and consciousness until he stumbled backward into the same crater his brother had fallen into. He tumbled to a stop, wheezing, fighting for each breath. Tears filled his eyes as he became crippeled with fear.

As he lay there, the barrage stopped. He realized that next to him was his brother. He desperately wanted to help him, but he could hardly move. He couldn't even tilt his head in that direction. All he could do was cut his eyes to the side.

Trent lay on his back. Hunter couldn't see his face. Their hands touched the way they had landed and Hunter used all the strength he had left to skoot his partially on top of Trents.

"Trent..I...I don't want to die," Hunter whimpered. Tears came from his eyes, but he didn't even have the strength to fully cry.

Here at the end, that was the only thought on his mind. He was terrified of what was coming. What was waiting for him there?

A dark chill ran down Hunter's spine. He heard footsteps. They grew closer. Hunter grew cold.

A soldier leaned over him. He didn't wear a helmet. He was young, maybe twenty, and had dark hair. He wore a black stone on his chest and black energy flickered across his body. His face was emotionless.

"Please," Hunter pleaded with all his might.

He was answered by the man lifting his hand over Hunter's chest and unleashing a torrent of the black energy. Instantly, Hunter was consumed by utter darkness.

Chapter 13

Hunter's muscles tensed, and his eyes jolted open. He took a sharp, deep breath. His muscles ached and it was difficult to move. His mind was foggy, and his brain throbbed.

It was dark, but his vision was so blurred, that was all he could tell. It was cold. He was laying on his back, arms sprawled out beside him just as they had been when he had fallen. He shuffled his hand across the ground beside him, searching for his brother. He didn't find him.

Finally, he built up the strength and the courage to push himself into a sitting position. This intensified his headache. He groaned and rubbed his forehead. It didn't take long for his vision to return. When it did, he found that he was in a small room.

The room was made entirely of concrete. It was only about eight feet wide and square, and the same on every side, except one side had a solid steel door. The only light in the room came from a tiny window, a slit with extremely thick glass that sat only about a foot from the ceiling on the back wall. From it didn't come daylight, but the light of the moon.

As Hunter looked around the room, flashes, memories began to play in his mind. He remembered the last few minutes he had been conscious: the fight, the crystal bearers, Trent, Brady, his parents. Hunter began to sob.

"Trent!" he screamed, as if he could hear him, as if he would come running to the rescue, "Trent!"

"Brady!"

"Mom!"

"Dad!"

The mention of their names broke him, for he knew their fates. "Dad," he cried, one last time before giving up. He hunched forward and placed his fists on the ground.

He wept bitterly for longer than he could keep track of. He swung from anger, to sorrow, to hatred, to grief, and back to anger over and over again, until he found himself utterly alone.

Alone, in a dark, empty room with only his emotions and his failures. If only they had run away without going to town. If only he hadn't waited so long to tell his family his secret. If only he had trained longer - trained harder.

He cried a bit longer, then found he had no more tears. He began heaving and coughed up bile. It was bitter and foul tasting. His throat and tongue burned.

When he felt utterly defeated, he scooted himself into the corner of the room, against the back wall, under the window. There he pressed his head against the wall.

He wanted to sleep. It would be his only escape. But sleep left him alone. He was left to stare at the emptiness of the room.

He stared till his eyes burned, till they were so dry they felt as though they were about to crack. It felt that every time, just before they shattered, his mind forced him to blink and started the whole process over again. And again. And again.

Sunlight never came through the window. People never came from the door. The room was completely silent with the exception of the sound of Hunter's beating heart, which he wished had stopped beating with the rest of his family's. Each beat was as if it were their ghosts haunting him.

This all went on just the same until Hunter was on the brink of starvation. His athletic build began to shrivel away into a sickly form. His once spoiled stomach demanded food, but received none. It retaliated by twisting in knots and growling constantly. It pained him; every second, the pain grew stronger until it finally exceeded the pain he felt in his heart.

His throat was dry and his mouth no longer produces saliva. His eyes no longer produced tears.

Then, there was a sound. It was so faint he didn't hear it at first. It came from the door. Then, there was a clanging. A twisting of gears. A robotic hum. The door opened, creaking as it slowly swung open.

Light poured in. Hunter squinted. Through the light was the silhouette of a man. It was a familiar silhouette because from its chest came a faint red glow. Hunter's nose curled at the realization, but he didn't have the strength to retaliate further.

"Good evening," he greeted.

Hunter said nothing. His eyes were adjusting now. The bearer wasn't wearing his helmet or armor or weapons. He was dressed in a long-sleeve, black uniform and tactical boots. He smiled pleasantly.

"I must apologize for your mistreatment," he said, off puttingly chipper, "Food rations are low. So is the staff. Actually, I must admit we're stretched a little thin right now. I hope you understand."

"What do you want?" Hunter croaked. His voice was all but gone and his mouth was bone dry.

"To offer you something better than this cell," the bearer said, taking on the tone of a businessman, "You have abilities that would be useful to us. I have a team of incredible people you could join."

If there was a way Hunter could hate this man any more, he couldn't find it. The nerve to ask Hunter to join *HIM*?

"I would never help you," Hunter growled.

"You wouldn't be helping me," the man countered. Even though he was trying to be persuasive, his voice still sounded menacing, "You would be going into cities that have been attacked and helping them recover, while offering them protection, of course. You would be saving families from catastrophes like the one that claimed yours."

"*You* are the catastrophe that took my family!" Hunter yelled, somehow finding strength to stand (though he had to lean on the wall).

141

"I am trying to save families!" the man yelled back. His eyes changed in an instant, going from soft to wild, "Whether you ever understand it, or not, I am doing what's best for this entire planet!" He walked toward Hunter and stooped down, placing his face in front of Hunter's. His hot breath fell on Hunter's cold face, "I'm giving you an opportunity to stay out of the war and in my good graces. I suggest you take it."

"Either kill me, or get out of my cell," Hunter grunted. Though his mouth was dry, he had somehow managed to produce some spittle. He gathered it together and blew it in the man's face.

Anger erupted across the man's face and a wave of his chaotic red energy rushed across his body. He shuffled backward and wiped the spit from his face, then straightened up and half-way composed himself.

"You're too valuable to kill," the man whispered through his teeth, "Your connection to that crystal is unique." He walked toward the door, then turned back just before stepping out, "You're going to be stuck here, wallowing in your filth. Growing old in this cell on the brink of death, until one day we get what we need from you, and I come here to kill you myself."

"I'll look forward to it then," Hunter snarled.

The man turned away and slammed the door behind him. When he was sure the man was gone, Hunter slid down the wall, back into his crunched up position.

He had been through so many emotions since he had been here, he didn't exactly know which one to pick for this occasion. He was almost too numb to feel most of them anymore, but hatred sounded like the most appropriate. It was one of the last ones he could feel.

It boiled in his chest and nearly warmed his cold body. It made him shake and drool. The audacity of this man to ask for his help. To think Hunter would even consider his offer for a second was an insult to his integrity.

Hunter made up his mind that he would never cooperate in their experiments. It wasn't long before he was given a chance to prove it.

A short time after the red crystal bearer left, the door began to clank again. It opened, revealing a short man in a white lab coat. He was older, maybe in his late 60's. What was left of his hair was white, but he had a bald spot on the top of his head that constrained his hair to the sides. Behind him stood two much larger men in their soldier uniforms.

"Stand up, boy," he demanded in a thick Russian accent.

Hunter did so slowly. He actually smiled a bit as he envisioned what he was about to do. He lifted his hands out in front of him, envisioning the energy of the crystal flowing over them, leaping off, and throwing the entire group against the grey concrete wall in the hallway on the other side of the door.

His anticipation faded as nothing happened. He tried again, pushing his arms forward. Nothing. Again. Nothing. Hunter looked at his hands distraught, searching for the problem. What had happened to his powers?

"Your stone is waiting for you, but your powers are of no use here," the short man informed, "Come with me."

Hunter refused, but the two other men forced him. They each grabbed one of his arms and drug him out of the cell.

The hall outside the cell was made of the same concrete as the cell. It was very long and lit by flickering fluorescent lights. They only went down a short ways before they came to an unmarked door on the left side of the hall. The man in the lab coat opened the door and the other men walked in. They closed the door behind them.

This room looked completely different from everything else. It was solid white and lit with bright lights. Every wall was identical, except for the one on the right, which was one big mirror. The floor was white as well, but had different cut outs in it where it looked like the floor could raise and lower.

"Now," the man said, looking at the mirrored wall, "Unrestrain his crystal."

143

Instantly, Huner felt the warmth of the crystal's energy in his veins. His aching muscles stopped aching. His headache subsided. His body temperature rose. The man looked back at Hunter, who was trying to conceal the transformation.

"Now, use your crystal's energy," he instructed, "Just allow it to flow across your body."

Hunter didn't respond. He only looked the other way.

"Otpusti yego," the man commended the soldiers restraining me.

The men released his arms and stepped back. Hunter looked back at the man. He reached under his lab coat and pulled out a piece of metal. It was cylindrical and appeared to be a handle.

The man lifted it over his head and then swung it down. From it extended a flexible metal wire. When it was extended, it smacked the ground and from it sprang blue electrical arcs. The air around it sizzled.

"Use your power," the man demanded.

Hunter's eyes were wide, and he backed away from the man. He was determined not to comply, but was filled with fear. The man flung the electrical whip through the air. It cracked just in front of Hunter. A blinding blue flash filled the room.

Hunter closed his eyes. He was ready to give in and do what the man asked. What was the point in resisting anyway? Then, in his mind's eye, he saw the face of his brother. He saw him in the driver's seat, taking him and his friends on their last great adventure.

Then, he saw the face of Austin. He saw the wonder in his eyes when they discovered the entrance to the hidden world.

Then, he saw Brady. He saw the fear and relief in his eyes when he popped up on the other side of the wall inside the hidden world.

Then, He saw Trent. He saw him cracking jokes as he and Hunter rode in the Jeep.

Then, he saw his mom. He saw the smile on her face on his first day of school, when she made him turn back to hug her.

Then, he saw his dad. He saw him standing in front of his family making a plan for them to be safe. He saw the determination in his eyes.

Hunter turned back to the man with the same determination in his own eyes, and gritted his teeth as he pulled back the whip.

Chapter 14

Every day, or what he assumed was every day, Hunter took his beating in the same manner. The two men would take him from his cell and leave him in the white room. The man in the lab coat would take out his electric whip and demand Hunter use his powers. When the request failed, he would beat, and beat, and beat, to no avail.

The lashes were excruciating because of the energy in them, but would leave no wound other than a red line on his skin. They never brought blood. They did sear through the fabric of Hunter's clothes, reducing them to shreds. Hunter couldn't figure out how they burned the fabric and not his skin, but then again, he didn't really care.

He would attempt to contain his screams in the beginning, but by the end of each beating, he would wail, and cry, and scream at the top of his lungs. It never changed anything.

After each beating, he would be dropped off at his cell and given a cup of water and a bowl of oatmeal, which he had to eat with his hands. At first, he considered not eating it. He wanted to starve, but the pain would grow too great. He figured the beatings every day for the rest of his life would still be less painful than starving himself.

This repeated itself on a cycle that Hunter assumed would never end. He was determined that they wouldn't break him. They were determined to break him. Neither of their wills were breaking anytime soon. Hunter thought he could come to terms with that. He couldn't.

***

The door of the cell creaked open and the two men appeared as they always did. Hunter stood. He no longer fought them. He just wanted to get his beating over with today.

Without a word, they walked down the hall as they always did, but today, something different happened. Coming down the hall was a young girl in a black uniform similar to the other soldiers.

Her hair was white-blonde and pulled into a tight bun on the back of her head. Her skin was a very pale white that almost looked to be slightly blue in the fluorescent lighting. On her chest was a crystal. It was a light, baby blue and shimmered like sunlight reflecting through water.

She turned just ahead of them and entered a room just up the hall, one door ahead of the white room. Just as the door closed behind her, Hunter was shoved into his room.

He wanted to think about who she was. Was she new or had he just never seen her before. What powers did she have?

These questions were quickly masked by something else new catching Hunter's attention. Usually the room was empty, with the exception of the man in the lab coat. Now, there was a large metal chair in the room. It was raised a bit off the floor and was quite stout. It had thick cuffs on both the armrests and the foot rest. Sticking out around the edges of the char were little nodes with circles of metal around them and a metal ball on the end. There were divots in the seat of the chair that concealed the same nodes.

"What's that?" Hunter asked, his voice shaking. He had adopted a sort of indifference to the whippings. Though they were excruciating and, some days, were almost enough to make him give in, he'd almost gotten used to them in a way. This was new, and looked much more scary.

To make it even worse, the soldiers said nothing. They only shoved Hunter into the char and bound him to it. Hunter's body trembled as they walked away and exited the room. The door slammed behind them and Hunter was left in silence.

He pulled at the restraints, but they were tight. He couldn't slip his hand out. He could only wait for something else to happen, which didn't take long.

"The chair is strong, but not stronger than your powers," the man in the labcoat's voice said over a P.A.

There was a hardly audible voice in the background, but the words were clear. It was a woman's voice, "You can't be serious." Followed by a "Shush," from the man.

147

There was a crack as the P.A. turned off and a low hum began to come from the chair. Hunter squirmed trying to free himself with his own strength. It was useless. He could only wait for the pain.

The chair's hum grew louder and louder, until red energy appeared on nodes lining the chair. They hissed as they prepared to strike.

Hunter squirmed more frantically now. His breathing was labored. This was the first time in a while he had felt true terror like he had the day he was taken.

"No!" Hunter cried, "Please!"

His plea was ignored. The red energy leaped from the nodes and raced across Hunter's body. The pain was the worst he had ever experienced. It felt as though his body were being ripped apart only to be put back together and torn apart again.

Hunter screamed and begged, but none came to his aid. Still, he refused to tap into his powers. He began to lose control of his movements as his body jerked this way and that.

Soon, he felt as though he couldn't use his powers even if he wanted to. His mind could focus on nothing else but the pain.

Then, it stopped.

Hunter slumped down in the chair, unable to move. Smoke rose from his clothes, or his body, he wasn't sure. The pain had left as soon as the energy had, but his body was ransacked from the experience. He sat there, his mind trying to recover as assess the damage.

Before he could even truly gain his senses again, there was a commotion behind the mirror, then a door slammed, then his door was flung open, so hard the wall it was connected to cracked when the door slammed into it. An icy breeze swept into the room

The white-haired girl stormed into the room, hurriedly followed by the man in the lab coat.

"I don't care what your orders were," she barked in her own Russian accent. She turned to face the scientist, "You will never do this again!"

"And would you like to take that up with the director?" the man threatened, "You have no authority here."

"Would you like to enlighten me on who the director is now that Darren's gone?" The girl yelled back, "I have the power to end your life with the wave of my hand." She leaned in, nearly presing her face against his, "That is the only authority that matters here."

A soft blue energy surrounded the woman's body. She lifted her hand toward the man and caused the teal energy to congregate there. It swirled around her hand like a blizzard. The man stepped back and his face turned pale.

"Get out!" she growled.

The man scurried out of the room and the girl walked over to Hunter. As she walked, her energy dissipated and her skin turned from paper white, to a more fleshy tone.

Hunter groaned in the chair, hardly able to move. The girl pressed a button on the back of the seat and the binders released. After this, she scooped Hunter out of the chair and sat him on the floor, propping him against the mirrored wall.

"Are you okay?" she asked.

"I think I'll live," Hunter whispered, for that was the only thing he could do.

"I'm so sorry they did this to you," the girl consoled.

"Then why do you work for them?" Hunter asked spitefully.

"The same reason you should," she replied.

This girl was strange to Hunter. Everything and everyone he had experienced in The Organization had been so crude, evil, and rigid.

149

She was gentle. She seemed good. She seemed like she wanted to do the right thing.

Their exchange was cut off when the two soldiers entered the room and stood at attention.

"Get him some new clothes and the best food you can find in this scum hole of a base," the girl commanded them. They left the room to fulfill her request and she turned back to Hunter, "Can you stand?"

Her accent made her intimidating, but her eyes were a soft blue, similar to the color of her energy. They held empathy and begged for Hunter's trust.

He didn't say anything back, but started to try and stand to his feet. The girl put his arm around her neck, put her arm behind his back, and lifted him to his feet.

His strength was quickly returning and the effects of the torturous chair were wearing off. He pulled away from the girl and stood on his own. He stared at the girl. She looked back, not even phased by his mental state. She looked back with compassion in her eyes.

"I don't know what gets into these people sometimes," she remarked, "They think they're saving the world, but they neglect people"

"Do you think you're saving the world?" Hunter asked mistrustingly.

"I'm saving myself," she answered, "And the ones I love."

Hunter gritted his teeth and scowled. He despised her for even mentioning the word love. What love was he allowed to have? "They didn't care to give me that chance," Hunter barked.

"For that I'm truly sorry," the girl said.

Even her compassion couldn't redeem her now. Only one thing could, "If that's true, then set me free."

"It's not that simple," the girl frowned, "I wish I could, but the only way for me to do that is for you to join us."

Hunter shook his head and walked past the girl, toward the door.

"Where are you going," she called after him.

"Back to my cell," Hunter replied, "If that's alright with you."

The girl didn't reply, and Hunter never looked back. He simply walked down the hall and entered his cell without a word. He reached for the door and slammed it shut behind him.

Hunter didn't see her or the man in the lab coat for a long, long while. He also never saw the soldiers. As a matter of fact, he never saw anyone. From then on, he was never tortured again. He was only exiled to his cell.

He was treated very differently now. Every day, more accurately, night, a woman in civilian clothes delivered clean clothes, three meals that included some kind of meat, and a tall pitcher of water.

His natural strength began to return to him now that he was on a steady diet with real food. Now, the only torture he was left to deal with were his own memories. Those and boredom. Really, they went hand and hand. When he did nothing, he cried, because the flood of memories would ransack his thoughts.

For this reason, he often found himself running in circles around the room, or doing jumping jacks and push-ups and other exercises, anything to keep his mind off of... everything. Sometimes, he questioned if he were going insane, but he didn't really have any other people off of which to gauge his level of insanity.

Then, one night, (though here, it was always night), the door opened. Hunter assumed it was his food, but instantly recognised the icy chill that filled the room. There, standing in the doorway, was the girl who had saved him.

"Hunter," she said, her accent made thicker by her shaky and frantic voice, "Your name's Hunter right? I need your help."

Hunter was a bit frustrated that she would even ask such a thing. More than that, he was almost hurt that she was just now returning. "Why would I help you?"

"Because I helped you" she pleaded. Her breathing was heavy and her cold energy leaked across her body. A tear slipped down her cheek. She was desperate.

He didn't exactly see what she had done as help, though it clearly was. His hatred for The Organization had blinded him to her sympathy. Still, he didn't know why, but her plea had persuaded him. He would at least see what she wanted.

"Fine," Hunter said.

As soon as he agreed, she rushed him down the hall to the same white room. Hunter was instantly stricken with fear. It had been so long since he had been here, and he didn't want to go back. He stopped outside the door.

"You'll be fine, I promise," the girl said, and she opened the door and walked in.

Hunter peeked in. Everything was different here now. A different part of the floor had risen up, creating an operating table in the middle of the room.

Standing around it were two other people, a bearer and the man in the lab coat. The bearer looked to be in his twenties and wore an odd looking grey crystal on his chest. It looked more like a shiny stone. It didn't really glow, but he was using it.

A sort of foggy grey energy came from it. It flowed down his arms, and, as it went, it slowly faded into the same light blue color that came from the girl's.

On the table was a young man; it was hard to tell his exact age. He was convulsing and screaming. He wore a tarnished black uniform that the man in the lab coat was desperately trying to get off of him. While he worked, flames would erupt from the young man's body. Before the flames could make it very far, the man wielding the grey stone would use the blue energy to quench it. Somehow, the two

152

energies mixed together and canceled each other out. They seemed to be attracted to on another like magnets.

"I brought help, professor," the girl said, rushing across the room. When she reached the table, the man with the grey stone stepped back and stopped using his powers. The girl then started using her own energy. She placed her hands on the boy on the table. Her energy spread across his entire body, and he stopped screaming. His body relaxed. He now only wheezed as he tried to catch his breath.

The man in the lab coat turned around, "Good luck," he said, throwing his hands in the air.

Hunter walked across the room and watched as the group worked. It took them a few minutes, but eventually they got the uniform off. It revealed a horrid sight.

The boy's skin had been heavily damaged by his fiery abilities. His entire body was covered with the volatile patterns of the energy where it had left behind oozing burns. The only thing keeping them from reigniting was the light blue energy that flowed across them. Hunter stared at the burns, actually feeling sorry for him.

A monitor next to the professor started beeping. "What is that," Amelia asked.

The professor looked up from the bag of medical supplies he was rummaging through. "His heart rate is slowing," the professor said.

The girl's face turned from despiration to panic. She looked over to Hunter, "I know that we've treated you horribly, and there is nothing I can offer you in return, but I need you to heal my brother." she looked at the boy on the table.

Hunter thought for a minute. He didn't want to help this girl or her brother. Even if he did, he didn't think he could. He looked too far gone, "No," Hunter said, turning back for the door, "There's nothing I can do anyway."

The girl moved to follow Hunter, but the boy on the table began to stir when her energy moved away from him. She placed her hands back over him and turned to plead with Hunter.

"If you had the chance to save your brother wouldn't you?" she called.

This filled Hunter with rage, "Excuse me? My brother died. He was killed by one of you. My hand sat on top of his as he lay next to me dying." Hunter felt tears falling down his face as he screamed each word louder than the last. "Do you know how many times I've thought since I've been here, how my powers could have saved him. But I couldn't, because one of your bearers kept me from saving him. So yea, yea I would save my brother, but I can't!"

Just as he reached the door, intent on returning to his cell, the girl made one last plea.

"Then why are you going to be the bearer that keeps me from saving my brother?"

Hunter stopped. The words cut him. This girl, no matter how she got here, had been kind to him. No matter how much this organization deserved pain, she didn't. He realized that if he walked out of the room, he would have become one of them without even joining their cause.

Hunter turned back to her, "I really don't know if I can save him," he admitted, tears welling up in his eyes, "It could kill him."

"He's going to die if we don't try," the girl said.

"Okay," Hunter walked back to the operating table. Everyone looked at him. "Send the professor out," he commanded, 'He won't be collecting any data on me if I'm going to help you."

"You heard him," the girl said, "Go release his crystal and leave."

The professor said nothing out loud. He only grumbled in Russian as he left the room.

"You need to put as many nutrients into him as you can," Hunter instructed the remaining bearers, "I only speed up what the body is already doing. If it doesn't have what it needs, he'll die."

154

"On it," the man with the grey stone said. He walked to the I.V. bag and poured something in. Then, He grabbed a kit from under the table. "I'll put in a feeding tube."

As he got to work, Hunter assessed the wounds, "What causes this?" he asked the girl.

"His crystal," she answered, "Us, we can absorb all of our crystal's energy. He can't. It would kill a normal person instantly, but he can absorb just enough to stay alive... So long as my energy is around to counter it."

"So how did all of this happen?" Hunter asked.

"He was on a solo mission," Amelia explained, her voice still shaky, "Usually, he has a quantum battery that's entangled with my crystal, but it became damaged. He had to fly back here without it functioning properly."

"Done!" The man said, "Feeding tube is up and running."

Hunter only now realized this was the only person he had met here that had an American accent. He only had a second to realize this because as the man spoke, Hunter felt the strength from his own crystal surge through his body.

"Just in time," Hunter said, he looked at the girl, "I'll have to go slow."

She nodded her head.

Hunter called the energy to his body. It surged across him with its graceful, green patterns. It felt good to use it again. He held his hand over the boy in front of him, and began his slow work.

He moved his hand up and down his body, hovering just above the wounds. With each pass they looked a bit better, but it would take a lot for them to look normal.

"I'm Amelia by the way," the girl said, "My brother is Lucas."

"I'm Ryder," the man said. He was now leaning against the wall, paying extremely close attention to Hunter's powers.

"I'm Hunter," Hunter said reluctantly, "But I guess you all knew that."

"It's very nice to officially meet you," Amelia said.

Hunter still didn't know how to feel about her. He felt like this could all just be a ploy to get him to join their team. He knew this would take a few hours, so he decided to see what he could learn.

"So, do I get to ask where I'm at?" Hunter asked, "Have I at least earned that?"

Amelia looked at the healing wounds of her brother, then at Ryder. He didn't acknowledge her with anything more than eye contact.

She looked back at Hunter, "You're on a top secret base run by what some call 'The Organization'. It's in Siberia."

"That explains the angry Russian professor," Hunter said, hardly believing he had made an attempt at humor.

Amelia cracked a smile, "Yea. I have to say, he's quite the pain, but he's the only one here that speaks English, so I put up with him."

"Your English is pretty good," Hunter pointed out.

"Yes," she answered, "My mother thought me when I was very young."

"Where'd you guys grow up," Hunter asked, making his detectiveing with small talk.

"Lucas and I are from Kazan, Russia, but our parents moved us to Switzerland when Lucas was born. That's where we grew up."

"What about you?" Hunter asked Ryder.

"What about you?" Ryder asked back.

156

The name came to him quickly, but attempting to say it was like yanking the scab off a sealed wound. He had to though. He had to give information to get it.

"Boulder," Hunter managed to choke out. Just the mention of it brought tears to his eyes. He continued quickly to keep from crying, "Colorado, just outside of Denver"

"San Diego, California," Ryder said, "Born and raised."

"How'd you find a crystal in San Diego?" Hunter asked.

"How'd you find a crystal in Denver?" Ryder coundered.

"You can't just counter all of my questions with questions," Hunter said.

"You answer mine, I'll answer yours," Rayder offered.

"Well I'm not answering that one," Hunter said. He felt like that was one piece of useful information he could keep from them. He didn't know why, but he knew the cave was important. It needed to stay a secret, if only in honor of his friends.

"Well, since it looks like you two have this locked down now, I'm gonna go get some food," Ryder announced, then left the room.

Amelia and Hunter sat in silence for a while. Both were paying attention to their jobs and neither wanted to give the other too much information to work with.

Hunter stared at the wounds on Lucas' body. They were deep and raw. Not one place on his skin was untouched. The patterns of the energy always looked so pretty when they flowed across Hunter's body, but in this form, the patters were hideous. They grotesquely twisted around his body like a fleshy vine that had rooted into the body of this poor soul. Hunter did admire his work, as they slowly and silently closed.

"Thank you," Amelia said, breaking the silence, "For doing this."

"Guess I just didn't want to become as evil as the rest of you," Hunter said, trying to be hurtful. He was almost mad at himself for helping as it was.

"You really think I'm evil?" Amelia asked.

"You work for evil people," Hunter said, "You help them keep doing evil. That makes you evil."

"Did I help them keep doing evil to you?" She countered.

"You mean to tell me you're tearing them down from the inside?" Hunter sarcastically asked, already knowing the answer.

"No...I"

"So you're not helping them gain control of the world?"

"Well, I-"

"Then that means you're working for them," Hunter said, matter of factly, "You're helping them grow. You're helping them be evil."

"That's not true, Hunter," Amelia said.

"Explain to me how it's not."

"I made a deal with them," Amelia sighed, "They were going to kill me and my brother and the rest of my family. I said we would work for them in exchange for protection and a life of being left alone after the war."

"So you made a deal with the Devil in exchange for your soul," Hunter accused.

"I made a deal with the Devil in exchange for the lives of the people I love," Amelia countered. Tears filled her eyes, "And I try to make a difference here when I can."

"But you know what you're doing is wrong!" Hunter exclaimed.

"They're going to win with or without my help!" Amelia explained, defeated, "It's better to be on this side than the other when that happens."

"You don't know that they're going to win," Hunter said.

"Then the other side will have mercy on my family," Amelia hoped, "Unless they're evil too."

Her comment brought them back into silence. They worked quietly for hours. Finally, the wounds were healed. The oozing, red blisters and bare flesh were gone. All that was left were scars and puffy pink flesh that covered him from head to toe.

Hunter allowed the energy to fade from his body and stepped back from Lucas, "All done," Hunter said grimly. He was actually glad that he'd helped, but now he had a connection to these people. That made hating them more difficult.

Amelia blinked out of a daydream. She examined her brother's healed wounds. A final tear slipped down her cheek. Saying nothing, she turned and gave Hunter a hug.

He didn't know what to do. The hug felt genuine, and it had been so long since he had one; he wanted to join in the embrace. But she had done too much. Though she had done good for him, the evil of working for The Organization was enough, in his eyes, to outweigh all the good. Though he only held his arms to the side, secretly, deep down, he enjoyed the hug.

Amelia let go and looked into Hunter's eyes, "Thank you, truly," she said, "If you ever decide you want to join…"

Hunter cut her off, "I think I'll go to my cell now."

He turned and walked out of the room. Amelia didn't come after him. He entered the hall and spied his open cell door a ways down the corridor and started the short journey he had taken so many times. As he walked toward it, he felt his connection to his crystal fade, just as he always did. However, this time, his mind felt a bit more free. When he reached the cell, he walked inside and pulled the door shut behind him.

Hunter didn't sit down in his usual corner. Instead, he found himself leaning on the door, getting a faint glimpse of the stars through the thin window. He found himself in thought.

He didn't know why, but they made him think back to the days when he was in Sunday school. He remembered, for some reason, the lesson of creation, how God made the stars of the fourth day. He couldn't figure out why he remembered that. It seemed like a rather obscure fact from the rest of the story. He couldn't even really remember what the rest of the days were.

He didn't ever figure out why his family stopped going to church. When he was little, they went every Sunday. He would always go to Sunday school. He actually really liked it. Then, sometime after he started playing baseball, they just stopped, or he and his dad did.

He guessed life just got "too busy". He would often have games or practices on Sunday's, and when he didn't, that was the only day they had off, so they spent it at home.

Even though Trent and his mom went, Hunter was just never interested anymore. He had even questioned if there was a God. How could that God they always said was so loving allow these things to happen? If he was so powerful, why didn't he come down here and do something about it?

That instantly reminded him of the Easter story. He couldn't help but wonder if all those stories were really true. The unknown seemed unproductive and just something else to clutter his mind. Maybe on a day when he had nothing to think about he could ponder it, but not right now. His mind was too busy focusing on the events that had just taken place. He just decided to look back at the stars.

As he looked, he thought about how many there were and how far away they were. He thought about how they still gave light to this place where the sun never shined. He didn't know how long this went on, but eventually his mind wandered to the vastness and complexness of the universe. He though about how truly small this place ws and how much he long to be out there - anywhere in that vastness but here. And, though he tried not to, that led him right back to thinking about God.

Debating the possibility and probability that there was a God, Hunter decided to try and talk to him, just in case there really was.

"Hey...um God..." He started, trying to think of how you should talk to such an entity, "Trent and Mom... and Brady too, used to say you know everything... and that you can do anything, but I'm just not sure about that. But if you really did come down here, and if you really do love me like they say you do, get me out of this place."

Hunter slouched down on the wall. He didn't feel anything happening. All that was on his mind now was the same thing that always was on his mind: the family he'd lost. A tear slipped down his cheek.

"You know what? Never mind. Those are just stories anyway." Hunter shook his head, disappointed in himself, and the God that didn't exist. He sat and stared at the wall.

Then, something did happen. A familiar warmth began to surge through his veins. The pain left his achy, sore muscles and joints. His cold, purple hands and feet returned to their normal color. Hunter knew what this was; it was his crystal. His connection was restored. But why?

He turned his eyes back to the stars, "Are you doing this?" he asked God.

He began to look around the room for his options. This could be a new ploy by The Organization to get him to use his powers. He didn't want to fall into their trap and give them what they wanted. Though he had just used his powers for the past few hours. What could it reall hurt?

There was the possability that this could be a power outage that was affecting whatever was disrupting his connection with the crystal. If that were true, he may be able to break through the wall of the cell, but he had no idea what would be waiting for him out there.

The other option would be to try and break into one of the adjoining rooms, but that would leave him in this building, trying to find a way to escape or hide.

Hunter's brainstorming was disrupted by the clanging of his cell door. Hunter scurried away and pressed himself against the far corner of the cell, prepared to attack whoever entered.

The door slowly creaked open and the light of the hallway poured in. The silhouette of two men appeared in the light. Where the men back to torture him into using his powers?

Hunter winced in anticipation of the iminent beating. He waited for the two to drag him out of the room. That never happened.

Instead, their metal helmets retracted around their necks, revealing young men, not much older than Trent was. One took a few cautious steps into the room. Hunter could now see that their uniforms were different. The uniform of the one staying back was grey and similar to the uniform of the other soldiers he had seen, but the soldier closest to him wore a white uniform.

On the right sleeve there were two purple bands. Above the bands was a metal pin depicting a dove whose wings stretched out in a flaming pattern, surrounded by a ring. Most notably, on his chest, was a puck like the one Hunter had owned, and in it, a glowing purple crystal.

The boy's eyes were soft, and he smiled nervously. He had curley brown hair, cut short around the sides. He looked kind.

The boy took a few gentle, cautious steps toward Hunter. Hunter didn't know what to do, so he just stood and waited for the boy to do something first. He did.

He stretched out his hand toward Hunter. His fist was closed around something. Slowly, he loosened his grip and opened his hand. Sitting in his palm was Hunter's green crystal.

The boy smiled and in a voice Hunter recognized said, "I think this belongs to you."

Hello reader,

I hope you enjoyed this story. Hunter Hogan's story will continue in The Crystal: Parts 4-6! You can find it and more books from Books for the Nations Publishing on Amazon.com. If you enjoyed this book, please leave a good review!

For special insights, book release information, concept art, and more, follow us on Facebook (Books for the Nations Publishing) and Instagram (@booksforthenations).

Thank you for your support.

For the Nations!
-J. A. Daniel